Saint Nicholas's Girls
D.P. McHenry

Throw Me A Kiss Publishing

ISBN: 978-0-9906959-4-3

To Norman; my daddy, my blue jay and my best
business teacher.

And to Susan, who led me to the mountain.

ONE

The Jay Feather Inn stood at the end of a long, winding gravel drive surrounded by tall pines and sugar maple trees. The entrance from the road was unassuming; no grand gate or lion statuary announcing you'd arrived there, just a simple white painted sign with the name and a carved blue jay. The drive itself was lovely as the sugar maples and birch trees formed a canopy over the gravel. The rough surface caused cars to slow, and once they slowed the vehicle's occupants began to appreciate the beauty of the property. On the south side was the river, which was either a trickle or a deluge depending on the spring snow melt and summer rain. A footbridge led to a dense wood with trails on the far side of the river. To the north was the Green Mountain National Forest with foothills and more trails leading to higher and tougher terrain. Behind the Inn was a beautiful old weathered barn. The Inn's distance from the main road made it a quiet and peaceful respite for all who entered, most coming in summer and fall for hiking and foliage. But it was late November, usually a quiet time between autumn and ski season in Vermont.

The town of O'Dell was within walking distance of the Inn if you liked to walk. Just about a mile down the mountain but not so steep a decline that the walk back was unpleasant. It made guests feel as though they'd earned the cookies or caramels that perpetually graced the sideboard of the great room. A quaint New England town, O'Dell had a village green, the requisite steepled white church, brick and stone town offices, colonial houses with wavy glass windows and enough shops and restaurants to keep visitors busy on a rainy summer day or when the clouds were low enough that the leaf peeping was obscured. But in late November visitors could feel a buzz in the town: not a rumble or an explosion, just a buzz. Christmas was coming and people in O'Dell did it up big. Houses and businesses were decorated in a tasteful old New England way. Garland around the lampposts and around the doorframes with a big, beautiful wreath on the door, a candle in each window and tiny white lights in the foliage. The mammoth pine tree on the village green was also lit. The powers that be at Rockefeller Center in New York had looked at the O'Dell village green tree as a candidate for their

Christmas tree overlooking the Rockefeller Center Skating Rink, but it had not made the cut. It didn't matter; the citizens of O'Dell would never have let it go. Understand that O'Dell was not averse to having trees from their town in other people's cities at Christmas time. The Roots and Sky Christmas Tree Farm and Nursery on the outside of town drew customers from 50 miles away because the trip was always worthwhile; hot chocolate while you picked and cut your tree, Santa's village on the green with both Mr. *and* Mrs. Claus (as well as some elves) in attendance to hear what the kids wished for, lunch at a the Buttery Scone Café, some Christmas shopping at Gigi's Closet, Tot's Toyland, and The Funky Table, and now, just this year, if you were making a weekend of it a night at The Jay Feather Inn.

The Jay Feather was not a hoity-toity destination resort. Simple, clean, a bit eclectic, always warm and inviting, it was a full country inn, not just a bed and breakfast. Both breakfast and dinner were included and there was a full bar with a good, solid wine list. And cats. Two of them; Peaches and Herb, a shout out to the owner's love of music, especially of old soul and R&B. They had the run of the common areas and the owner's suite, but at this time of year spent most of their time in front of one of the fireplaces or under the wood stove. Literally, under the stove. Herb would get as low to the ground as he possibly could and shimmy his fine self between the stove's legs and then roll onto his back to absorb the radiating heat onto his buff colored belly. Kitty nirvana. Peaches preferred a nice soft pillow with no theatrics, just a walk and a plop, followed by a contented sigh as her eyes closed.

When people came to The Jay Feather Inn they felt as though they were coming home. Even if they had never visited before they felt a comfort they couldn't explain – like they were in the house they wished they'd grown up in; warm, cozy, loved. Faith Nicholas knew how to take care of people, and how to nurture the Christmas spirit all year. Her mother gave birth to her on Christmas Day 1981. The nurses suggested Noelle, but her mom thought it too common for a Christmas baby, and way too trite for a child with the last name of Nicholas. Noelle Nicholas? Seriously? She didn't want her child being referred to as Santa's kid. She'd have enough trials and tribulations growing up with a single parent. And probably get screwed on birthday gifts being

7

born on Christmas day. What she would need would be faith. So Faith she became. Not that her mom was overly religious, quite the contrary; she was a lapsed Catholic having a child out of wedlock with no father in the picture. This kid was going to need lots and lots of faith. And hope, and luck, and love.

Patty Nicholas was 18 when Faith was born. She had gone to Ireland on a school-sponsored trip and fell in love with a boy from her great grandmother's village, the son of the publican. She was a totally inexperienced babe in the woods and he was a coal eyed Irish charmer, he smoldered like a peat fire. He was just her age and just as inexperienced, but they'd figured it out. She'd kept in touch with him until she'd found out she was pregnant. She had no idea what she was going to do but didn't want the complication of the baby's father who might not agree with her choice. What choice? Her parents didn't give her one, really. She graduated high school with a wicked case of morning sickness and was sent to her father's best friend on Cape Cod until the baby was born. Patty could have given the baby up for adoption but once she saw her she couldn't even imagine not keeping her.

Patty's parents understood. They helped support and care for the new mother and child, and Patty eventually finished college with a degree in hotel and restaurant management. So with both parents either in or from the hospitality business Faith's innkeeping was literally in the blood. She grew up following her mother from hotel to hotel, spent summers with her grandparents and great-grandmother, and dreamed of a place she could call home for more than a couple of years as her mother climbed the corporate ladder. Her mother taught her how to make people feel special, her grandmother gave her spunk, her grandfather taught her about people and business and how caramels were the best candy in the world, and her great-grandmother taught her to cook. She had great summers camping on a lake, Christmases with birthday cake, but no father. She was happy. She asked his name once and her mother told her, and Patty told her Faith looked like him; dark eyes, dark hair, pale, freckled skin. Patty even saw some of the same mannerisms – the exaggerated head tilt and furrowed brow when asking a question, the way she wiggled her fingers when excited about something, but she never told Faith that part. She enjoyed seeing him everyday in her daughter, even if he was just a teenage romance. And Faith never asked about her father again. When people asked *her* she said she didn't know him, and then changed the subject.

It seemed natural that Faith would also choose hospitality. She *was* a natural, and had connections through Patty for internships during the summer and job offers upon graduation. And while she chose the corporate world initially she knew in her heart that she really wanted a smaller, more intimate innkeeping experience, so she saved her money, lived frugally and dreamed of her own place. A place she could call home, a place she wouldn't have to leave after a year or two because a new position opened up for her mom, or lately, for herself. When her beloved grandfather died she received an unexpected inheritance. He detailed in his will how the money was to be used for her inn or small hotel, and had his lawyer connect her with financial advisors who could guide her through the process.

Finding the inn was the next project. There were many bank owned properties that had been bought by couples who had no idea of the amount of work involved, or had no grasp of the hospitality business. They thought it would be fun, a lark, something to keep the missus busy while hubby commuted back to New York. One banker called those "A very expensive mistake". Some were for sale by older owners who'd had a good run but one of the couple was ill and couldn't continue to do the work, or they had let the property fall down around them. Faith was not sure she wanted the bad karma of a failed business or a failing innkeeper, so she continued to look.

One weekend while Faith was taking a break from her search she visited her mother in Manhattan and they happened upon a psychic fair in Union Square. On a lark they sat together for an angel card reading, not knowing what to expect. The reader described Faith's grandfather to a tee, and looked Faith in the eye and said, "You're trying to by an Inn." Patty fell back in her chair as Faith leaned further forward.

"How did you know that?"

"Your grandfather told me."

"Go on..."

"He said to give you this." The reader reached into her bag and after rustling around for a bit pulled out a blue jay feather and handed it to Faith. "He said this was the key to the right one, and it's in central Vermont. In the Green Mountains."

Faith took the feather and felt it's softness and it's spine. Just like her, just like her mom. She looked over at Patty, who was softly crying.

"I miss him, honey." Patty whispered.

"Me, too, Mom."

"Oh," said the reader, "He said to tell both of you… he's tired of being the only guy in the family and don't give up on men because he was such a pain in the ass." The card reader's eyes opened wide, surprised by her own comments. Faith and Patty's heads rolled back as they laughed.

"He used to tell us that all the time!" Patty said.

"Now we're sure it's him!" Faith added, wiping her eyes.

Back at her mother's apartment Faith Googled "Blue Jay Inn Vermont". Fifty pages of Vermont Inns popped up. She tried "Central Vermont Inns for sale". A bunch of commercial real estate sites appeared, some with which she was already working. But further down the list was a site for an inn that was for sale by owner.

The Jay Feather Inn, O'Dell, Vermont
jayfeatherinnforsale.com

For Sale or Rent by Owners – 18 room inn with ski lodge, not currently being run as an inn. Owners have opportunity to teach LEED and sustainability courses nationally and will be unavailable for renovation and day-to-day operation. Please contact Jerry and Tanya Grant for more information.

Faith's heart beat a bit faster as she wiggled her fingers. The ad might as well have read "For Sale with Good Karma". She clicked on the link. The Inn was an old colonial, built around 1800, and the current owners had lovingly cared for it, even though they were only using it as a house. Faith could see necessary updates were required, but the important things were in order; as long as it had good bones she could work with it. She called the number listed in the ad.

Jerry and Tanya Grant were welcoming and gracious hosts. They had asked Faith and Patty to stay with them to get a sense of the place while they discussed the possibility of the sale. As it turned out Jerry and Tanya had two children and fostered many more in their time at The Jay Feather, which was why they never ran the place as an inn. The ski lodge was used to house out of town school teams when there were meets at the local ski area, as Jerry was a coach and their oldest was on the high school ski team. Tanya worked part time at The Roots and Sky Christmas Tree Farm and full time as a mom while blogging on sustainability. Jerry was an engineering professor who taught LEED certification courses. This opportunity, now that their kids were all grown and fairly settled, was too good to pass up. They'd be on the road much of the year and wanted to significantly downsize. Their oldest son had a house in O'Dell and was the new owner of Roots and Sky; his rambling farmhouse had plenty of room for a suite for his folks, so it was time to sell.

Faith explored and photographed every room, every nook and cranny of the place, inside and out. She envisioned the changes and renovations, wondered if all the fireplaces would meet code, and in her mind's eye saw the ski lodge filled with families and lots of kids. The energy of the place was good. The town was beautiful and the shopkeepers and business owners were all welcoming. For so long the area lodging was an old motel outside of town, the chain hotels in Montpelier, which was too far away, or the slope-side ski resorts, which were too pricey. The locals wanted a place they could call their own, where friends and family could stay for a local wedding or at Thanksgiving and Christmas, where travelers could lodge for the O'Dell Christmas Festival. Not to mention how Inn-to-Inn hikers and bikers would bring extra business to the town. Faith was feeling good about the place but was still a bit jittery about spending $500,000 on a place with no business. In essence she was buying a house; creating the business was up to her. She shivered a bit while inspecting the inside of the walk-in cooler so Tanya handed her a fleece jacket to put on, one she kept outside of the door for when she was putting away groceries. Faith put her hands in the pockets and felt something paper wrapped. She pulled out a caramel, one that was a favorite of her grandfather's.

"How did that get there?" Tanya asked. "I don't even like caramel."

Faith chuckled. "My grandfather is telling me I'm home."

TWO

Faith knew she would buy The Jay Feather, but even her confidence and determination didn't ease the butterflies she felt about having to renovate *and* build a business with no income stream. Her grandfather's money and her own savings gave her enough to buy the place, and, if she was very cost conscious, do most of the renovations, but then what?

"Mom," she asked Patty, "Do you think I can make this work?"

Patty had a glow about her that Faith hadn't seen in a long time. Her strawberry blonde hair was caught up in her usual chignon, which Faith thought made her mom look older, but today she had rosy cheeks and her hazel eyes were bright with excitement, making her look like a girl.

"Faith, honey, I see so much potential here. Casual, comfortable, homey... That's it, it feels homey, like a place people will really want to stay in."

"But will I be able to do everything that needs to be done AND get business going before I run out of money?" Faiths fingers wiggled.

"The universe always provides..."

Patty was a big believer in universe handouts, a window opening when a door closed, everything happening as it's supposed to and all that. She had to. She raised a child by herself, certainly with emotional support from her parents and grandmother, but she'd paid back every cent of every loan for college, housing and anything else her parents had provided. She was independent but she'd had some exceptional luck, and now because of a solid career in the hotel industry for 25 years and a high-ranking position at Classic Hotels of the World she was in a position to BE THE UNIVERSE. 401k, savings, good investments in both stocks and real estate would allow her to provide a safety net for her daughter and maybe even provide her with the solid home base she had been unable to before.

"Let me help you with this, but not unless you need it. Buy the place, but talk to Grandpa's financial guys and see if they'll allow you to take a loan against your investments so you don't have to deplete your funds. Money is cheap right now; if you can keep your cash for the renovation and repay the mortgage over time you'll have enough to get the business going. And I'll be able to loan you whatever you need if you run over on the renovation."

The words tumbled out of Patty's mouth so quickly Faith barely kept up. Faith had seen this excitement in her mother before. New hotel startups really got Patty's juices flowing. Her mother was the Tasmanian devil of organization, a visionary in her field who ran circles around both her management and subordinates.

"Let me show you what I found in the ski lodge."

Patty led Faith to a storage area in the barn turned ski lodge. Tucked into a corner was the original Jay Feather Inn sign. A carved Blue Jay on an antique wooden board whitewashed and painted with black lettering. Blue, black and white paint colored the jay. It was a bit dinged up and would need some repair, but it was in one piece.

Faith showed her mother the caramel she'd found in the fleece jacket's pocket.

"Grandpa says go for it." Patty smiled and nodded.

Faith had spent the time leading up to the closing date interviewing contactors and making plans for the renovations. Only half of the rooms had ever been used regularly, the others occasionally or not at all. They were on the smallish side and some shared a bath. Faith knew every room would need an en suite bath and that some would need to be enlarged. She had plans for a bridal suite, a two bedroom family suite, and knew which walls would need to come down to provide the extra space and baths for the remaining guest rooms. She had realized the Inn would end up with 15 rooms vs. 18, but her business plan still worked and the bankers all approved it. The owner's suite was fine, big enough for her, her mom when she visited, and the cats. There was a small office behind the check-in desk, but an Innkeeper should hardly ever be in it anyway, so that was okay. The great room was beautiful with a large stone fireplace, wide pine floors, large windows overlooking the river on one side and the mountain on the other. The dining room had beautiful wainscoting and wood beamed ceilings, and a fireplace with a large wooden mantle – perfect for Christmas decorations. Adjoining the dining room was the old tavern room. Faith could see where the new bar would go and how she'd arrange it as a welcoming and cozy lounge. It would have a perfect view of either of the great room or dining room's fireplaces, so no one would feel like they didn't have a perfect seat. There was a library with a fireplace and inglenook, perfect for meeting with clients planning special events.

The biggest problem was the furniture was pretty much all going to need to be replaced. Many years of active kids that turned into rambunctious teenagers had taken their toll, and the Grants were taking any newish pieces they had purchased with them for their apartment at their son's home. Faith knew what an uncomfortable bed or a shabby sofa could mean in an on-line review, so along with new linens, comforters, and towels she was sourcing new mattresses and armoires, sofas and chairs for the common areas, and barstools and cocktail tables. She would have some pieces refinished, and source hardware and bathroom fixtures from renovator's warehouses, hopefully for a fraction of the cost of new. Thankfully the large kitchen didn't need much. Some minor adjustments to the plumbing and a fire suppression system to get up to code, but that was it. The huge walk-in cooler, freezer, icemaker and old Viking stove were all in working order. The counter tops were stainless steel and there were stainless racks in both the kitchen and the butler's pantry. But her favorite feature was the woodstove. It was in the corner in a bowed window that was full of shelves for herb plants and flowerpots; it would keep them toasty as they wintered inside. Such a treat it would be to be able to grow her own herbs year 'round.

Faith knew she was lucky in that the Inn had not been operational since the onslaught of social media; no bad reviews, upset guests or wedding disasters would haunt her as the new owner. But she needed to get out of the gate quickly with a great website and some great press to help her. She had a friend who would do the website, and the Grants had photos of the Inn during every season. She'd use some stock photos of Vermont, write the verbiage and she already knew which reservation software management program she wanted to buy. Done.

The press would be harder. She started by contacting the local paper to let them know her plans.

Jack Kimball was the owner, editor, advertising salesman, and reporter for The O'Dell Weekly Times. It was basically a one-man show. He was a native Vermonter and had inherited the paper from his father. He'd been running it for 20 years, but did it because he loved it; he didn't need the money. His family had owned the largest ski area in Vermont before a big investment firm bought it out. As old, frugal Vermonters their businesses and homes were all paid for, so the influx of cash allowed them to either retire to warmer climes, as his parents had as Vermont was not kind to their 80 year old bones, or in Jack's case run a paper that barely made ends meet while being able to volunteer on the fire and rescue squad, tutor junior high school kids, and coach the ski team with Jerry Grant.

Jack was aware Jerry and Tanya were selling their place, so was not surprised that the new owner would be interested in talking to him. But he was surprised that the thirtyish raven-haired beauty that walked into his office was she. He introduced himself and they sat down.

"Welcome to O'Dell."

"Thanks, Jack. Is it OK if I call you Jack?"

"I'm gonna feel really old if you don't."

Faith smiled.

"I know I don't actually own The Jay Feather yet, but we're on schedule for the closing in August and I was wondering if I could get you to run a press release. Just something talking about me, my background, what I have planned for the place... You know, the usual. I'm going to need to hire some help and I'd like to mention that as well. Oh, I guess I should take out some want ads, huh?"

"Don't bother, nobody ever reads them. Go on our website and you can do it for free, and they update daily. Faster that way. And try Craig's List, too." Jack smiled.

"Did you just screw yourself out of some ad revenue?" Faith asked.

"Just being realistic. Do you have the press release written or would you like me to interview you?"

"I just happen to have one..." She grinned at him.

"Ok, let me have a look." He scanned the page. "Are you doing this by yourself?" he looked up over his half-frame reading glasses.

"Yes. I've been in hospitality since college, and my mother is a director at Great Hotels of the World, so I come by it honestly."

"No husband?" His eyebrows rose.

"Nope. No time for one. This has been my dream since I was a kid."

"What does your father do?"

"No idea. He's not in the picture."

"Is your mother single?"

"Is that pertinent?" Faith narrowed her smiling eyes.

"Sorry. But I'm guessing she's my age, and if she looks anything like you I'd love to meet her." Jack chuckled.

Faith laughed. "Are YOU single?"

"Yup. Divorced actually, a very, very long time ago. No kids."

"Hmm. I'll trade you an introduction for a really great article..." Faith grinned. "Full disclosure; she's strawberry blonde, sort of the antithesis of me. So if you're expecting a dark eyed brunette you're going to be disappointed."

"If you learned your negotiating skills from her I might be frightened. Interested, but frightened."

Faith laughed. Jack was a handsome, outdoorsy kind of guy. His blond hair was going grey, and was little long in the back. He had a ruddy face and a strong chin, and blue eyes that crinkled at the corners when he smiled. He seemed like a nice guy. Maybe she would make that introduction.

"So who do you need to hire?" he asked.

"Housekeepers, a sous chef, waitresses, a bartender, a maintenance guy slash landscaping guy... Possibly an assistant. All part time at first until we get up and running."

"Bartender? Full bar?"

"Yes, I've been told by the town a permit wouldn't be a problem."

"Great! Folks have been looking for a place to go after work. The big inn down the hill in Whitman frowns upon us hicks taking up space at their establishment."

"Something I should know about the locals?" Faith's eyebrows rose.

"Nah. We're mostly a good bunch. We're more jeans and snow boots to their khakis and penny loafers. It's a bit stuffy down there." Jack gave his Thurston Howell impression, which made Faith laugh.

"Mostly?" she asked.

17

"Every town has a few… shall we say interesting characters? O'Dell is no different."

"Well, I want The Jay Feather to be comfortable and welcoming, and I'm not imposing any dress code, so come on up. I guess I'll take my chances with the 'interesting characters'."

They talked a bit about life in general, and life in O'Dell and when Jack shook her hand he really meant it when he said it had been a pleasure to meet her.

The O'Dell Weekly Times came out a couple of days later.

"The Jay Feather Inn Reopening Under New Ownership." Faith read out loud. Not only had he used her press release but he had embellished it, adding his own spin. He mentioned she was hiring some part time help, and that the Inn would have a lounge open to the public.

"The new owner, Faith Nicholas, is a lovely young woman who will be a great addition to the O'Dell social scene." Faith's eyebrows rose. This really was a small town. He also included her telephone number. Soon thereafter her cell started to ring. Faith screened out a few lonely locals looking for dates, the ladies that wanted just a few hours when their kids were in school, but not the hours Faith needed *them*. She had a couple of interviews lined up for a housekeeper as well as for a bartender/assistant manager. They looked promising.

Iris Parsons was an O'Dell transplant. She'd come north from New York after a guy, and while the guy hadn't worked out Iris fell in love with the area and stayed. Artistic, flamboyant and charming, Iris was a crack barkeep and a whirlwind of efficiency. She was a potter who sold her wares at local gift shops and artisan's workshops, but it wasn't enough to pay all the bills. Besides, Iris was way too social to stay in her studio, just her and the kiln. She needed to be around people and was great at schmoozing customers. Tiny, just 5'2", and a waif, she had curly blonde tresses that had their own zip code. She tamed them into a floppy knot on the top of her head that gave her an additional 3 inches of height. Faith liked her instantly but was a little concerned about getting her to wear the uniform: black pants and a white oxford with the Inn's logo on the chest.

"No problem, I'd actually prefer it. That way I don't have to think about what to wear. Sometimes I can dress sorta out there and you might have to reel me in. This is *much* easier!"

Faith smiled. She asked Iris to make two standard cocktails and something of her own design. Iris made an excellent Bourbon Manhattan, an outstanding Side Car, and an awe inspiring Ginger Martini. And was certified to pour a perfect pint of Guinness. Hired.

Rita Levinson was an earthy 60ish grandmother with funky earrings and a long graying braid. Her husband was the history teacher at the high school and they had a small property up behind Roots and Sky. She originally stopped by to find out if Faith would like to buy eggs from her free range chickens for The Jay Feather, but when she ran into Iris on her way out the door Iris told her Faith was looking for help so Rita inquired.

"I'm looking for someone to do breakfast service and clean rooms, and I'm also looking for dinner servers. Would either be of interest to you?" Faith asked.

"Well, yes, I think so... I used to be a chambermaid here when I was a teenager. Now my youngest grandchild is in school so I'm doing less babysitting than I used to. I'd have time certainly. And I could use some extra cash for Christmas presents. My kids all bred like rabbits. We only had three but they each had four. I can't keep 'em straight half the time. And one of my granddaughters is a sophomore at the High School; she might be interested in waitressing at night. "

Faith asked around and found out Rita was a straight shooter, a hard worker and ran a tight ship at home, which was always immaculate. Kendra, her granddaughter stopped by later that day and was equally as impressive. She'd worked the lunch shift at The Buttery Scone summers and school breaks and was saving for college. She said she could handle both jobs and could start whenever Faith needed her. Hired and hired.

Delroy Naismith applied for the job of sous chef. He was a Jamaican lad who had graduated from the New England Culinary Institute and fallen in love with a local girl, Taylor Levinson, another of Rita's granddaughters and Kendra's cousin. Taylor was still in school and had another year left, so Delroy wanted to stay around to be near her. He had short dreads and when he cooked kept them under a knitted cap the colors of the Jamaican flag. He was tall and lanky with a huge grin and a quick wit, and he charmed Faith right from the start.

"What do you like to cook?" she asked.

"I can cook anything, boss lady. You tell me what to cook and I cook it."

Faith smiled and enjoyed his Jamaican lilt.

"I didn't ask what *can* you cook, I asked what do you *like* to cook."

"Ah, ya mon, I see. I love spices, I love to cook jerk with rice and peas. It remind me of home."

Faith loved jerk *anything*; chicken, pork, it didn't matter.

"OK, here's the deal. The kitchen is yours for the afternoon. You should find everything you need to make jerk chicken, and I'm going to give you one of my recipes for an appetizer and a side dish. My mom and I will dine on your meal tonight and I'll make my determination then. You in?"

"I will do it, but be warned my jerk really should marinate overnight..."

"I'll take that into consideration. Better get moving," she smiled. He grinned and sauntered into the kitchen. Faith hoped he was good. She could afford him, for one. And straight out of culinary school he'd be a big old lump of clay she could mold into her chef. She wiggled her fingers.

Wilson Grant was the owner of Roots and Sky. Will was tall, rangy and looked more like a surfer than the mountain man that he was. His brown unkempt locks made him look sexy even though he never tried to be, and his blue eyes completed the package. He and his Akita named Hank lived in the farmhouse at Roots and Sky with his brother Tom, and soon there would be an apartment in one wing for his folks. Jerry and Tanya's eldest son had done what his parents requested. He finished college and got an MBA but his heart wasn't in the corporate world. He wanted to grow things and make things. He was an expert woodworker, finish carpenter and cabinetmaker who was kept busy with renovations and special projects when he wasn't tending to his Christmas Tree farm. Roots and Sky's busiest time was between Thanksgiving and Christmas, but the summer and fall were hopping as well. Will rented out the retail space to the farmer's market co-op and they kept a permanent stand open from June to late October with seasonal vegetables and fruit as well as mums, pumpkins, apples and their famous apple cider donuts in the fall. It was mostly hands off for Will, unless there was a pothole in the gravel parking lot or a plumbing issue in the store. Roots and Sky's trees required some year round work; pruning, fertilizing and the like, but his brother Tom mostly handled that.

Tom Grant was the youngest of the Grant clan and had been diagnosed with Asperger's very late in high school. He had been a brilliant but socially awkward student, and like his brother was interested in hands-on work even though he had college bound grades. After much deliberation he settled on Vermont Tech's agriculture program where he could attend but still live at home. Tom could make anything grow and was totally focused on his charges, whether they were Christmas trees or petunias. He was the foil to his brother; shorter, darker haired and dark eyed, more like his mom than his dad. Will always looked out for Tom, even though Tom was pretty self-sufficient. Will was afraid Tom's difficulty with eye contact might be mistaken for shiftiness, and coached his brother before important events and anytime he was within eyeshot of Iris. Tom had a crush on Iris since she came to O'Dell five years ago, and thought the guy she'd come with was a total jerk for leaving her. He always got nervous and tongue tied around her, and Will would try to help him shake it off.

"Look her in the eye and smile. 'Hi, Iris.' That's all you have to say. She's nice, and you know she's always been nice to you. Nothing to be afraid of, Buddy." Will would pat Tom's shoulder as he spun him in Iris' direction. And Will was right; Iris was always nice to him. But he had to do more than say "hi" and he could never seem to pull it off. So the crush's vice tightened.

Jerry and Tanya mentioned that Faith was looking for a contractor and a landscaper to Will and Tom. Will was encouraging Tom to get some private landscaping clients so he could branch out a bit more. Too much time alone on the tree farm wasn't such a great idea, and he could help pay a few more bills. So the brothers made their way "home" to meet with Faith. They found her winding up a phone interview with someone from AAA. She smiled at the brothers and motioned for them to sit at the table to join her.

"Yes, we close on the property next week and I plan to be open in a month, some rooms anyway; there'll be renovations for some others... Sure, please do a visit that week, it'll be a soft opening and you can establish a listing for me... I know you have to do a surprise visit for the ratings, that's fine. We'll be ready... No, thank *you!*" She ended the call and looked at the brothers. "You gotta be Tanya and Jerry's kids."

"Guilty," Will said. "I'm Will and this is Tom."

Will had prepped Tom to shake hands and make eye contact. But he forgot to smile.

"You look like your folks!" Faith was actually nervous. Why was she nervous? God, Will was handsome! She wiggled her fingers under the table.

"Yeah, we get that. We're here because I heard you were looking for a landscaper."

"I've heard Tom is the go-to guy for anything plant related. I was going to find you to find out if you were taking new clients."

Tom looked around nervously. "Yes, I am actually. I know this property. I planted most of the perennials, and the shrubs and bulbs, too."

"You did a great job. I love the plantings. Would you put annuals in for the summer? What are your thoughts?"

Tom immediately launched into a gardening plan, detailing what he'd plant, what colors he'd use, how he'd do new window boxes and plant a cutting garden so they'd have fresh flowers for the inn. All the while he was looking anywhere but at Faith. She looked at Will with an amazed look and Will grinned and winked at her. She felt her blood buzz. She asked about costs and they came to an agreement for a service contract where Faith paid a monthly fee and wholesale for the materials through Will and Tom's suppliers.

Faith took Tom's hands. He looked up at her nervously.

"Tom, I think you're going to do beautiful things here and I'm so happy we're going to be working together." Tom smiled.

Will asked Tom to wait for him outside, and Tom was happy to go look around the yard.

"Thanks for being so great with him. He has some issues with, well, meeting new people."

"*He's* great. My pleasure, really. He's so sweet and obviously loves the work."

22

Will realized at that point that he was not only attracted to Faith but that she was racking up points for humanity and kindness. Not something he saw a lot in strangers interacting with his brother.

"I also understand you're renovating. Have you found a contractor?"

"Not yet. We can open with 12 rooms but the renovations on the others will probably have to happen during regular business. Before I go broke." She smiled.

"I'd like to bid on the job."

"Can I afford you? Your mom showed me some of your work and it's gorgeous. And looks really expensive."

"Well, I was one of the guys that wore this place out so how 'bout I give you the friends and family rate?"

"Are we friends?" She grinned. Oh, God, she was flirting.

"I'd like that." He smiled and his eyes twinkled. "Show me what you have planned and I'll quote it."

"Here," she handed him a roll of paper from the table, "the drawings are all there. Take it home and look it over. And if you have any suggestions as to how to do it better please let me know."

"I'll do that. And I look forward to coming back with my quote." He tucked the roll under his arm and took her hand in both of his. "It was a real pleasure to meet you, Faith."

"S-same here," she stammered. Why was her heart beating out of her chest? This was VERY inconvenient! She had way too much to do! She watched Will go out and head to the truck with Tom. She realized she was watching his butt.

"Who's your friend," she called.

"Hank," Will yelled. "Go see Faith," he directed the dog with a tilt of the head. The big Akita trotted up the stairs and sat obediently in front of Faith. She let him sniff the back of her hand before rubbing his head and scratching him behind the ears. He rolled over, paws up. She rubbed his belly as he let out a happy sound, sort of a "roooooowl". Will laughed.

"You've made a friend."

"What a love-muffin," she smiled, "does he like cats?"

Patty and Faith sat in the dining room enjoying a glass of wine and catching up on the week's events. Patty was pleased Faith was ramping up on staff so quickly, and was delighted when Delroy placed a soup terrine with an appetizer of top neck clams, chouriço, and peppers flavored with white wine and cumin in front of both of them. He stepped back and in Top Chef fashion described the dish, the preparation and wished them irie instead of bon appétit. They dug in. Faith looked at her mom and they both grinned.

"This is better than mine. He put something else in here. What is it?" Faith asked her.

"I think maybe he used vermouth instead of white wine. Happy accident?"

Delroy came back to the table, and they asked him.

"So, here be the ting," Delroy said, "you had no white wine in the kitchen, but you had vermouth. I think vermouth give everything a richer taste, and it reduce down betta."

"Nicely done, Delroy."

He next placed a beautifully plated jerk chicken with rice and peas. Faith's recipe was for a side of ratatouille, which came on its own plate garnished with sautéed plantains.

"I didn't think I had plantains in the kitchen... What did you use? Green bananas?"

"Sometimes we have to improvise, boss lady."

Faith and Patty feasted on Delroy's beautiful meal. When they had all but licked the plates Delroy cleared and brought them tea and dessert.

"Dessert! Delroy, you didn't need to make dessert."

"Just taste, boss lady."

Faith dug into an ice cream of amazing depth. Cinnamon, allspice, ginger and what? Something subtle. Coconut? The mouth feel was different.

"Did you use coconut milk?" she asked.

"Ya mon."

"Delroy, you are hired."

"Irie, boss lady, me mash it up."

THREE

Will came back with some really innovative suggestions and a really cheap price.

"Why are you doing this?" Faith asked, her head tilted.

"Because I can. Roots and Sky is doing well, I'm between big jobs where I'll make a pile of money, and truth be told I have ulterior motives." He grinned at her. She blushed.

"So," she tried to deflect his attentions, "when can you start?"

The closing went smoothly and a whirlwind of activity began at the inn. Guest bathrooms were renovated, rooms painted and floors were refinished in no time flat. Patty was in town to help, and all hired hands were on deck as the kitchen was scrubbed and brought up to Board of Health code, and the deliveries of new beds and bedding, refinished furniture and supplies arrived. Tom was in heaven as he had a reason to see Iris every day and could easily talk to her about what he was working on when she'd sit on the porch during her break. She'd ask him about the flowers and for the first time she began to appreciate how passionate he was about his work. Iris knew about the Asperger's, most everyone in town did, but in this tight knit community they took care of their own, and Tom was treated like everyone else. Iris had heard that people with Asperger's could be violent, but she'd seen nothing but gentleness from Tom, and a bit of discomfort with eye contact. He was polite and a gentleman, a bit intense when it came to any kind of flora but that wasn't terrible. And it was obvious that he liked her. She didn't quite know what to do about that, and quite frankly, neither did he.

Early one morning Faith stood in the kitchen alone, drinking coffee and looking up the mountain. She could just make out the logging road on the edge of her property. There were sugar maples on her land. She wondered if she could find someone to tap them for syrup. How cool would that be? She could serve maple syrup from her own property. A flash of black on the logging road disturbed her reverie. A truck pulled up and stopped. She could make out a man emerging from the cab. Tall, with a receding hairline and a ponytail. He walked around the truck and out of her line of vision. She shrugged; he wasn't on her property. She went back to her cup of coffee and the punch list she worked on daily. Lost in thought she jumped when someone knocked on the kitchen door. She opened the door and the man she'd seen get out of the truck was leaning on the doorframe. He slowly gave her the once over, while chewing on a toothpick. Faith felt like she was standing there naked, and reflexively folded her arms across her chest.

"Can I help you?" she asked, noticing a snake tattoo that wound around his neck and ended on his cheek. The snake's mouth was open with a flicking tongue and long fangs. She had to stop herself from shuddering. He was handsome in a dangerous way; he had dark, penetrating eyes and a fierce look about him.

"More like can I help you?" he replied. Faith wasn't sure where this was going. "You the new owner?" he asked. Faith went for professional instead of skeeved out.

"Yes. Faith Nicholas." She extended her hand. "And you are?"

"Rex Buckley. Folks call me Buck." He took her hand and held it a little too long. She had to pull it away. "I come to find out if you have a source for firewood yet."

"Um, no, not yet."

"That coffee smells good," he motioned his chin toward her cup. Faith now had to decide whether she was going to make a friend or a foe, and Buck looked like he could be a formidable enemy.

"How do you take it?" she asked, opening the door to let him in.

"Lotta sugar. Helps my disposition," he mumbled. She almost laughed. She prepared his cup, feeling like he was undressing her with his eyes as she did. She turned and handed it to him, keeping eye contact. She wasn't going to ask him to sit.

"You a logger?" she asked.

"I do a lotta stuff. Jack of all trades."

"On the up and up?" She gave him a look that told him she wouldn't tolerate illegal activity.

"Mostly."

"Well, at least you're honest."

26

He nodded.

"I'm running a legitimate business here. I'm not going to risk it buying bootleg from you. So what's your story?" she asked.

"Got me a woodlot up the mountain. I got dried stuff from last year I can sell ya, and I'll cut and dry stuff for next year at a discount if you order it now and gimme a deposit. All legal."

"And the not so up and up part?" she asked.

"Well, lets say sometimes I get shipments of stuff and I can't tell ya where it comes from. But its good stuff. Needs a home, and I sell it. Sometimes its food. Electronics. Depends on what's out there."

Faith wondered if she should do business with this guy just to stay on his good side.

"How much for two cords?" she asked.

Will had walled off the rooms that were to be totally renovated so he could keep down the dust and the noise. Once the inn was open he planned to work on any of the noisy stuff after breakfast or when Faith gave him the all clear that the guests were all up and about. He'd set up his saws and materials in the barn to keep the real racket away from the main building, and he was going to suggest they turn the barn's loft back into a dorm-like ski lodge, where Faith could put up visiting ski teams without them running amok in the inn. He was hoping for a lot more work from The Jay Feather, not only to make his old home a beautiful place for travelers, but also to get to spend more time around Faith. She'd been haunting his dreams at night. Hell, he spent most of the day thinking about her. They had flirted, and she seemed a bit flustered around him at times, but he was going to take it slow. She was opening a brand new business and he was smart enough to know the inn had to come first. If he moved too fast she'd refuse him, and he didn't want that to happen. He'd work to be indispensable to her inn and maybe she'd trust him with the other parts of her life. His dog, Hank had already become a fixture, following Faith around and getting to know the cats, Peaches and Herb. Hank already had his own water bowl in the mudroom. During the hubbub the big Akita and the cats were all in the kitchen by the woodstove, out of the fray.

27

Faith had hoped the inn would have a soft opening but Dan Churchill from the Vermont Inn to Inn Biking and Hiking Association had contacted Faith on a tip from Will Grant. He had groups of hikers and bikers that would love a stop in O'Dell, never having had a place to stay in town before, so her soft opening turned into an almost full house. And the townspeople were all chomping at the bit for the bar to open and for a nice place to have dinner.

Iris was setting up the bar, Patty was directing delivery traffic, Rita was cleaning bathrooms and making up beds, Delroy was taking in food deliveries and organizing the walk-in cooler, and Faith was checking bills of lading and writing checks when Jack Kimball strolled in. Patty was dressed for dirty work in jeans and a tee shirt with her hair in a ponytail, and had a smudge on her forehead from fireplace ash.

"Can we help you?" she asked. "We're not open yet I'm afraid."

"Is Faith around? I'm Jack Kimball from The O'Dell Weekly Times."

Faith had told Patty about Jack wanting to meet her. She wasn't really interested and she was sure her countenance today would certainly scare him off. But he *was* kind of cute.

"Sure, she's in the Tap Room going over invoices." She led him into the bar. Faith looked up.

"Hi Jack! I see you've met my mom." Patty was behind him making the universal don't-go-there sign to Faith, waving her hands side to side and shaking her head. Jack turned around as Patty dropped her hands and smiled her most charming smile.

"THIS is your mother? Sister maybe, but not mother," Jack chuckled as he shook her hand.

"Sorry about the mess," Patty gestured to her clothes and hair, blowing a strand off her forehead, "I'm Patty Nicholas."

"So happy to meet you." Jack hadn't let her hand go.

Another truck pulled in with a furniture delivery and Patty excused herself. Jack turned around to face Faith and Iris, who were both smirking.

"You OK Jack?" Iris asked.

"Can I get a drink?" He looked like he needed to sit down.

Iris and Faith chuckled.

"Iris, fix him his usual, whatever that is."

Iris pulled out a bottle of Glenlivet and a rocks glass as Jack took a barstool.

"So, how are things going?" Jack asked after he took a swallow. He kept looking toward the great room to try to get a peek at Patty. Faith chuckled.

"We should be open on Wednesday and we have 9 rooms booked for Friday night."

"Wow. Ok if I put that in the paper?"

Faith nodded, grinning.

"When will the dining room be open?" Jack pulled out his notepad and began jotting in it.

"Wednesday as well. I was hoping to get a few tables in for a couple of nights before the hikers hit on Friday. But *please* tell people to call for a reservation if they want to come right after we open; I'd hate to have a mad rush the first night. Also, write that I plan to have a grand opening party in a couple of weeks and everyone will be invited. They can taste the menu items then."

Jack nodded, "Ok for them to come for a drink before then?"

"Absolutely."

"Put me down for 3 people for Wednesday night at seven. Jerry and Tanya are still here and I know they'd love to see this."

Faith jotted down the reservation in the book. She sighed a long sigh and looked at Jack.

"Can I ask you something?"

"Sure." He sipped his drink.

"Tell me about Buck."

Jack winced. Iris shook her head.

"Is that everything I need to know?" Faith asked.

"Do you remember when I told you about our 'interesting characters'?" he asked. She nodded.

"He'd be one of 'em, complete with a scary tattoo."

"A pain in the asp?" Faith quipped.

Jack threw his head back and laughed.

"Depends," he said. "How'd you meet him?"

Faith recounted the circumstances and their conversation about cord wood.

"You're fine buying wood from him. Tanya and Jerry did, I do. I'd steer clear of the rest. He's a slippery devil. Gets

29

away with a lot but isn't, shall we say, unknown to the police."

"He threatened to come and frequent the bar. Am I going to have a problem there?"

"He'll probably be your best customer. Good news is he's a pretty mellow drunk. And he's a great storyteller, so he'll lend some local color. He does do some long haul trucking so he's not always in town. It sounds like you've already set some ground rules with him. Let him know in no uncertain terms that he can't go behind the bar and help himself, and he has to use the front door. He'll help himself to food if he comes and goes through the kitchen. He lived here for a bit; he was one of Jerry and Tanya's foster kids."

"Really?"

"Yup. His folks had a cabin up in the woods, poor as dirt. His dad would leave to find work and his mom would take in laundry. Proud. Didn't want welfare or food stamps. It was what did her in. She made sure Buck was fed and she starved herself. She got the flu one year and it killed her. No one knew where his dad was, so Tanya and Jerry took him in."

"How'd that go?"

"It was hard. He was thirteen. He wanted to be out on his own. Couldn't understand why he just couldn't stay at his cabin and make his own way. He ran away a few times, got into trouble. He was the only one of Tanya and Jerry's foster kids they ever had a problem with. Finally his dad came back and took him to stay with an aunt in New Hampshire. As soon as Buck was old enough he came back and reclaimed the cabin and the woodlot. His dad was gone and he left it to Buck. None of us really know how Buck manages to eke out a living, and we don't ask questions."

"Kind of sad, isn't it?" Iris asked.

"Well, I guess I'll go with the flow on this one, and hope he doesn't become a problem for me." Faith shrugged.

"Good plan," Jack replied. "Hey, can I walk around to check out what you've done with the place? I promise I won't get in the way."

"Sure," Faith smiled, "she's probably upstairs telling the mattress company where to put the beds."

Jack blushed. "Thanks. Maybe I can make that reservation for four." He took his drink, notepad and sheepish grin toward the stairs.

30

Jack remembered what the inn had looked like as a private residence and the transformation was breathtaking. The colors were soothing and modern but the furnishings and fixtures gave the place a comfortable, woodsy feel. Furniture placement was interesting and lent itself to people easily conversing while still having beautiful views out of large windows that overlooked the river or the mountain. The large stone fireplace was the centerpiece and its mantle had been polished to gleaming. Antique crossed snowshoes hung above the various sized ivory pillar candles. Jack could see how stunning the effect would be. The guest rooms maintained the color scheme and the newly renovated baths with walk-in showers with river stone floors, stone colored tile, glass shower doors and square sinks were knockouts, really top notch. White, fluffy towels and robes and white bed linens and duvets over down comforters made the beds inviting. Faith had really done an outstanding job. Rita was finishing up one of the rooms as Jack stood at the door.

"What do you think Jack? Gorgeous, isn't it?" she asked.

"Just incredible. I had no idea."

"That girl is amazing. Wait 'til you taste her recipes!"

"That good?"

Rita just nodded with a wistful look on her face. "That young man in the kitchen is a hoot. He's seeing Taylor. Did you know that? Sweet guy. Delroy's his name."

Patty was showing the movers the way to the stairs and stuck her head in.

"Do you like?" She asked Jack with a smile. Poor Jack liked on so many levels. Rita headed to the next room to get started on the new bedding there.

"Your daughter has done a beautiful job and I think we should celebrate her good work. I'm bringing Jerry and Tanya for dinner on Wednesday. Have you been shanghaied into service or can you join us?"

Patty looked surprised. This guy worked fast.

"Wow. Um, I was planning to be around if she needed me but I guess if she doesn't..."

"Good. I'll tell her to up the reservation. And you're here if she does need you. Seven o'clock OK?"

"Yeah, fine." She was smiling as he trotted down the stairs.

31

FOUR

Faith and Patty took one last walk through the inn before they opened the doors for business. Tom had provided beautiful cut flowers for the common areas, tables and bar. Iris and Kendra looked sharp in their uniforms. They had 4 dinner reservations staggered between seven and eight PM, so Iris could play maître d' as well as tend bar, and Patty would be free for what Faith and Iris were calling her "date". They had teased her unmercifully all week.

"It's beautiful, Sweetie," Patty squeezed Faith's hand. "Now get into the kitchen and see how your dinner prep is going."

"Hey, who owns this place, anyway?" Faith chided as she strode off into the kitchen smiling.

At 5 PM Will and Tom came into the Taproom and sat at the bar, each having Iris pour them a Longtrail Lager draft. Buck walked in and stood in the entrance to the Taproom, thumbs hooked in his pockets. He looked around. Tom looked over at Will and tilted his head toward Buck. Will turned. He and Buck made eye contact. They both nodded once. Buck made his way to the bar and sat a few seats away from his foster brothers. He ordered a draft beer. Kendra brought fresh, homemade potato chips with a chunky maple ketchup for them to munch on with their beers. Faith came out of the kitchen shortly after in her chef's whites to say hi. She was surprised to see Buck at the bar. As she approached Will and Tom he looked at her and nodded.

"Yowza, Faith. These are awesome," Will grinned as he tossed another chip in his mouth. "We may stay for dinner!"

"Your mom and dad are coming in later with Jack. I can have Iris put you all at a bigger table..."

"What, and spoil Jack's date with your mom?" Will whispered as Tom put his finger to his mouth in the hush sign as he glanced around nervously. Faith laughed.

"So I guess the whole town knows?" she asked.

"Pretty much," Tom replied.

"Where's Patty now?" Will looked around.

"Primping, of course. What do you think we girls do before dates?" Faith teased.

33

"You don't need to, Beautiful." Will whispered before he could stop himself. Iris' eyes went wide as Faith blushed. Buck raised his eyebrows. Tom inadvertently came to the rescue.

"I think you're both beautiful," he said, looking wistfully at Iris, and just as quickly looking away. Faith put her hand on his back.

"Thank you, Tom." She gave him a kiss on the cheek. He blushed. She then went to Will, and before he could react she grabbed his head in both her hands and gave him a kiss. A low moan escaped his lips.

"For good luck," she smiled as she walked back into the kitchen.

"Wait. What just happened?" Will asked, looking around. Buck's face grew stormy. Iris burst out laughing, and giggled all the way to the dining room entrance as their first reservation walked in.

The dinner service went smoothly. Faith had limited the reservations so as not to overtax her staff or herself on the first night. Delroy performed like a dream. Will and Tom did stay, but they ate at the bar, and several townspeople came by for a drink. Buck was quiet. He stopped and acknowledged Tanya and Jerry on his way out; they shook his hand and asked how he was.

Jerry, Tanya, Jack and Patty had a fabulous dinner with lots of laughter, and Iris got to open the first bottle of Champagne for the occasion. And the second bottle as well. Faith joined them as they finished up dessert and they, Will and Tom toasted to Faith's success.

Tom asked his parents for a lift home as he had an early day tomorrow, and Will hung back for a chat with Faith before he headed out. They walked into the barn so he could show her something he'd made for her. When he turned on the light there was an easel in front of her holding a plaque that read The Jay Feather Inn, Faith Nicholas, Proprietress. It was an oval sign with carved letters and an ogee edge. The sign was painted the colors of the inn and was sized appropriately to hang next to the front entrance. Faith gasped.

"Oh, Will! This is beautiful! How did you...? When did you...?"

"At home at night. I didn't want you to see it. I wanted to give it to you on opening day and if you liked it I could hang it before the Grand Opening."

"Like it? It's fabulous. And incredibly generous, like you haven't been generous enough. How can I ever thank you for everything?"

"I told you, I have ulterior motives." And with that, against all of his best-laid plans, he took her into his arms. She let out a little gasp and smiled.

"Listen Faith, I know you have a business to get off the ground and that's going to be your main focus. But I can't stop thinking about you and I'd just like to say I'll be here if and when you think the time is right. So until then I'd just like to give you something to think about."

He leaned in and kissed her, gently at first until she responded, but then he pulled her close and his kiss was hungry. She wound her arms around his neck and felt the stress of the day melt away. She kissed him back, feverishly and with abandon.

Patty and Jack had a nightcap at the bar. Their evening had been lovely; they had traded job stories and Tanya and Jerry had regaled Patty with tales of Jack's high jinx as ski coach over the years. They were comfortable in each other's company and Patty noticed he spent the night looking at her. Every time she caught him he smiled a lovesick puppy smile. It was obvious he was smitten. Patty wanted to be careful not to break his heart, as she was heading back to the city after the grand opening party and wasn't sure she could manage (or he would want) a long distance relationship.

"So, can I see you again?" Jack asked.

"Be pretty hard not to in a town this size," she quipped. He smiled.

"I'm not above resorting to blackmail; see me again or the inn gets a shitty review."

Patty laughed. She was pretty sure Jack didn't have that in him.

"I surrender."

"How about I cook dinner for you at my place?" he asked.

"Deal. When?"

"Friday?"

35

"Hmm. Faith's got almost a full house this weekend. Sunday would be better…"

"Sunday it is." Jack took her hand and kissed it. "Thank you for a lovely evening."

"My pleasure! Thank you for dinner."

Patty walked Jack to the front door. She gave him a hug that he returned by lifting her off the ground. She laughed.

"See you on Sunday," they said to each other.

FIVE

The weekend went smoothly. The Inn-to-Inn Hiking Association guests were lovely and they loved the inn. Patty suggested that if they were happy with their stay they not only tell all their friends but to be the first to write reviews on Trip Advisor or the travel site of their choosing. And most of them complied, giving Faith several five star reviews she could quote on the inn's website. During the weekend both Faith and Patty noticed each other smiling a great deal of the time. Was it the successful soft opening? Or was it something else? Will perhaps? Or Jack? The thought made them each smile more.

Faith knew she should be focusing on the inn exclusively, but she had replayed that kiss Will laid on her in her mind a thousand times since Wednesday. He'd been a gentleman. He knew she had other priorities but he'd let her know he was around when she was ready. How unbelievably gentlemanly was that? And he was around; all the time in fact, as he was trying to get her rooms finished and to start work on the ski lodge before the festival. He hung the plaque, his beautiful gift to her, by the front door for all to see, and everyone knew who had made it. They'd take it slow. They would get to know each other much better but without complications. Somehow there were always complications, but this was the good stuff, the heady, lusty, newness of unveiling the layers of another: the expectation, the discovery. Slow down and enjoy it, she told herself.

On Sunday afternoon after the guests had all checked out and Rita had finished up the rooms Faith found her mother in the kitchen frosting an Italian pound cake. It had been filled with ricotta cheese, grated chocolate and fruit and she was slathering on a chocolate ganache.

"I love that recipe," Faith said. "It looks great. What's the occasion?"

"I'm going to Jack's for dinner tonight."

"Are you, now?" Faith smirked.

"Hey, I'm not the only one whose been smiling since Wednesday night." Patty chided as she swatted Faith with her dishtowel. Faith blushed.

"I don't have time for romance right now, mom."

"Neither do I. So what? Aren't we entitled to some fun? Your grandfather thinks so."

"I'm more worried about Jack than you," Faith kidded. "Don't break his heart. I still have to live here after you traipse back to Manhattan."

"I don't traipse, Sweetie."

"So what are you wearing tonight? And will you bring me a piece of cake?"

Patty and her chocolate cassata cake showed up on Jack's doorstep at seven, Patty wearing jeans, a silk blouse and strappy sandals. Jack was so taken by her hair loose around her shoulders he could barely talk.

"I brought dessert, I hope you don't mind. I couldn't show up empty handed."

"Its beautiful," he said, not really even noticing the cake. "Come in, come in!"

Jack's house was an old colonial in town, with wood rubbed to shining and worn by years of use. It was obviously a bachelor's pad with nail head detailed leather furniture and masculine decorations. A wood duck decoy, photographs of the various ski teams Jack and Jerry coached over the years, two vintage Ski Vermont posters in dark wood frames, a wall of books, and a taxidermy rainbow trout over a stone fireplace were part of a nicely styled and cozy living room, and a breakfront with beautiful crystal liquor decanters and two matching glasses graced the dining room. The table was set with cloth napkins and good china, and pillar candles were flickering next to a vase of sunflowers. Patty could see Jack in the kitchen putting the cake on the counter. She followed him in, looking around at what looked to be the original cabinets and worn wooden countertops.

"Wow," she said. "How old is this kitchen?"

"Old, and the cabinets are sound. Didn't see a reason to change them."

It was charming. The kitchen had a door leading to a small patio, where lanterns were lit and a grill was heating up.

"Would you like a glass of wine? Or a drink?"

"Wine would be lovely," Patty replied.

"Red OK? We're having steak. A safe bet for most guys."

"Perfect," she laughed.

38

Jack grabbed a very impressive bottle of Cakebread Cabernet.

"Oooh," Patty murmured appreciatively. "That's one of my favorites."

"Then we're off to a good start." He decanted the bottle through an aerator.

"You're a wine guy."

"I do like a nice bottle. I'm dreadfully impatient with letting it breathe though, which is why I bought this thing." He pointed to the aerator. "But I've also been known to buy some cheap stuff, let it gasp for a minute and drink it." He smiled a goofy smile. They clinked glasses.

"Shall we sit outside for a bit?"

"I'll follow you," Patty said, savoring her first sip. Once outside Patty could see a tidy, well-maintained yard, with hydrangea bushes and hostas, daylilies, rudbeckia, purple coneflower, sunflowers and bee balm, and some sedum plants. "Are you a gardener?"

"Nah. I have Tom do it. He loves it and is so good at it I couldn't possibly imagine anyone else doing it."

"Did he cut the flowers for the table?" she teased.

"Nope, that was me." Jack blushed.

They sat at a small patio table where Jack had laid a simple plate of cheese, crackers and grapes. Patty wasn't sure how confident a cook Jack was but he was certainly making an effort.

They made small talk and when the conversation got a bit deeper he finally asked about Faith's father.

"Were you and Faith's dad ever married?"

Patty chuckled. "That would be a no." She told him about her Irish school trip.

"So she's never met him?"

"No. She's only really ever asked about him once. She asked his name and I told her. That was it."

"Any you've never spoken about it again?"

Patty shook her head.

"So how is it a gorgeous woman like you has never married at all?"

"No time. When I decided to keep Faith..."

"Keep her?"

"Yeah. My parents initially wanted me to give her up for adoption. I couldn't do it. So when I knew I'd be raising my kid alone I kind of went into overdrive. I went to college and grad school…"

"MBA?"

"Yup. Jumped into business with both feet, paid my parents back for my education, and started working my way up the corporate ladder. I know it was hard on Faith. We moved a lot as I changed jobs and got promotions. Thankfully my folks gave her some stability. They took her for the summer every year; they'd camp on Cape Cod and I'd come for a week to spend my vacation with them. And we'd all be together for Christmas. Between work and Faith I barely had time to sleep and get the occasional haircut, never mind have a relationship."

"So no dates?"

"Very few. Generally guys would get antsy as soon as they found out I had a kid. How about you? No one special after your divorce?"

"Hmm. Small town, slim pickings." He smiled. "I did date the occasional new teacher at the high school, and I had a wild fling with the girl's ski coach from Lake Placid, but as soon as I found out she was married…"

"Oh, no."

"Yup. Not my style. And she was too far away anyway."

"So, single, handsome and totally available?"

Jack blushed again. He shrugged, sat back and crossed his ankle over his knee. She nudged his foot with her toe.

"We might have to do something about that," she smiled slyly as she looked at him from the side of her eyes. Jack could feel his blood pressure rise.

"I think the grill's hot." He headed toward the kitchen as Patty chuckled.

Will and Hank drove up the hill to the inn. Hank's head hung out of the window and when they got close he started his happy whine: kind of a cross between a howl and a yip.

"You're as pathetic as I am," Will said to the dog.

A couple of cars were in the parking lot; Will recognized a few townspeople's vehicles and noticed an out of state license plate. Business was obviously good. He and Hank hopped down from the truck and Hank made a beeline

40

for the door. Will opened it and Hank immediately found Herb, the big yellow tabby, and gave him a bath. Will knew the two of them would be asleep in a soft spot together before long. He headed to the bar. He noticed Buck at his now usual spot. Dan Churchill was waiting for him at a table near the window, already sipping a local draft beer. Will motioned to Iris for the same and joined him.

"First time you've been in?" Will asked him.

"Yup. Far cry from when you and I were tearing this place up. Did you have to patch up that hole we made in your old bedroom?"

"Its one of the rooms under renovation. I don't think anybody's seen it; its been behind a mirror for about 15 years now."

Dan laughed. They were meeting to begin conversations about this year's O'Dell Christmas Festival. Will and Dan were on the committee this year and hoped to hash out some of the detail before they met with the bigger group. In years past they'd found it handy to have ideas at the ready or the group would pontificate for hours and not get a blessed thing done.

"This place is going to be packed," Dan said as he looked around.

"Faith'll be ready. That's why she opened up so fast. She wants to get her legs under her before the season starts. Fall *and* winter. I bet I can get her to do an ad in the brochure... maybe even a tie-in on the website."

"If she keeps getting reviews like the ones my Inn-to-Inn guests are writing on Trip Advisor I don't think she'll need to advertise. Unless, of course, there is more to your relationship than meets the eye..." Dan had an eyebrow raised and a grin playing at his lips. Just then Faith came from the kitchen with an appetizer platter and put it on the table between the two men.

"Iris told me you guys were here. I just wanted to say hi, Dan, as we've only spoken on the phone. And say thanks for the business."

Dan's eyes glazed over a bit looking at Faith. He managed a "My pleasure," before Will spoke.

"Thanks, Beautiful. Can you join us? We're talking about the Christmas Festival. My friend across the table here will come out of his stupor in a sec. He gets that way around hot women. Dude. Snap out of it."

41

"I won't stay if I'm going to be a distraction," Faith giggled.

"Sorry," Dan said. "You are not what I expected, and I mean that in a really, really good way."

"Thank you," Faith blushed. "So, Christmas Festival..."

"Uh, yeah. We run a page on the town's website and post it on the Facebook page, but we're thinking about a color brochure for the local businesses and rest areas. Kind of pricey, but if we get enough businesses to defray the cost it isn't too bad." Dan showed her last year's flyer.

"Nice. I'd need to know what the actual costs are before I could commit, but I'm interested. Could we do links between the websites as well?"

"Sure." Will mumbled with a mouthful of food. "These are great, by the way."

Dan dug in to a mushroom and cheese strudel.

"Wow. Would you be interested in a booth at the festival?"

"Don't you have other food vendors?"

"Jacob at the Buttery Scone is flat out with breakfast and lunch during the festival, so no, we don't have anyone doing it right now. Unless you include the hot apple cider and cider donuts at Roots and Sky."

"Hmm. We don't do lunch here, so we might be able to swing something. How about a winter soup or a nice stew? With French bread. Or better still we can put the stew in mini boules." Faith thought out loud, head tilted and fingers wiggling.

"Perfect," Dan said. "Can we let the committee know you're in?"

"Yeah. I think so," Faith nodded. The phone rang and Iris called her over. "Excuse me gentlemen, it seems I have a call. It was good meeting you Dan." She shook his hand and walked toward the office.

"Whoa," Dan whispered wistfully.

"Off limits, dude."

"Are you...?"

"Not yet. She's got a business to get going. We're taking it slow..."

"Lucky bastard."

Patty enjoyed every last bite of the top sirloin Jack had grilled perfectly for her. That was one thing about both

42

Patty and her daughter; they loved to eat. Patty and Jack tucked into her Italian cassata while coffee was brewing.

"Delicious," Jack looked up from his plate.

"Glad you like it." Patty smiled.

When they finished they took the plates into the kitchen.

"Faith threatened she wouldn't let me back in if I didn't bring her a piece. I hope you don't mind."

"Well, lets see. If you can't get back into the inn you'll just have to stay here..." Jack reached over and pulled Patty into his arms.

"Then what happens?" she asked.

"Should I tell you or show you?"

"Show me," she said breathlessly.

Jack's kisses were gentle and teasing. He kissed her lips and her neck, and made his way back to her lips.

"Should I show you more?" he whispered.

"Mmmm... yes."

He surprised her by scooping her up into his arms and carrying her to the hall.

"Sofa or bedroom?" he asked.

"Would you think badly of me if I said bedroom?"

"I'd think badly of me if you said sofa."

"Bedroom," Patty giggled.

He placed her gingerly on the bed and sat next to her.

"It's been awhile," he said.

"Me, too."

"So we can be awkward together?" he smiled.

"Lets go for it," she whispered, wickedly.

And soon they were tearing each other's clothes off. She thought him strong and sexy, he thought her soft and beautiful. They looked, they touched. Gentle caresses became more feverish, a stroke caused cries of pleasure, a kiss, a lick sent shivers.

"Now," she pleaded.

With that he entered her, slowly, gently until her raspy moan gave him permission to take her fully. They moved to each other's rhythms in an erotic dance. Their breathless kisses turned to desperate pants, and she couldn't suppress the sound of her climax. He followed soon after, not able to hold back, taken by her passionate cries. They collapsed together on the bed, happy and spent.

They caught their breath. She looked up at him and smiled, kissing his chin.

"OK?" he asked.

"Oh, more than OK," she whispered.

"Good. Faith doesn't really need cake tonight, does she?"

Patty and Jack's romance and Faith and Will's *friendship* were great fodder for the grapevine. Everyone was happy for Jack, who everyone agreed had been alone too long, even though Patty would soon be going back to Manhattan. She'd certainly be back and forth, but could they sustain this long distance liaison? And Will spent an inordinate amount of time at the inn, he usually ate dinner there a couple of times a week. Many of his business meetings were held in the lounge. The town looked at them as a perfect couple, if they ever became a couple. Faith was so busy with the inn she barely had time to sleep. Everyone could see the way they looked at each other. Someday, they all thought, that cauldron is going to boil over. But what everyone was currently talking about was the inn's grand opening party for the town. No one would miss it and the excitement was making Faith a little nervous. She was glad her mom was around until after the party.

A large tent had been raised outside the lounge, close to the barn. Will and Tom and cleared away Will's tools and building materials, and tidied up the space for overflow from the tent. The party was on a Sunday afternoon, rain or shine they were covered. Tom had taken some of his potted chrysanthemum stock and placed them in old milk buckets and funky containers he found in the barn. Iris helped him by mulching them with a bit of hay and tying blue bows around the pots and buckets. The effect was charming and rustic. Tables and chairs were set up café style, with white tablecloths and fresh flowers cut by Tom and arranged by Patty. Will delivered and stacked some hay bales to act as the outdoor bar, and Iris was busy placing trays of glassware, coolers, wine and a large glass beehive that would hold the signature punch they were serving for the party. It had bourbon and apple cider, a bit of ginger liqueur, some cinnamon, and ginger ale for effervescence.

The weather cooperated and the afternoon of the party was cool and sunny. With no breeze the sun felt warm and made for a perfect fall day.

Faith was planning an opulent buffet. Sure, there'd be some casual appetizers and nibbles at the bar and on trestle tables around the venue, but no carving station or heavy hors d'oeuvres tables where no one's satisfied because they feel like they haven't eaten a meal. The chafing dishes were at the ready with maple glazed pork tenderloin, sage and fennel stuffing, Delroy's famous jerk chicken, butternut squash lasagna, wild mushroom topped polenta, roasted root vegetables, arugula, corn and tomato salad and caramelized onion focaccia. For dessert she'd made an occasion cake, as pretty as any wedding cake, carrot with cream cheese frosting under a layer of fondant, decorated with The Jay Feather Inn's logo. And Delroy had made his incredible coconut spiced ice cream. Everything was beautiful.

Faith wore a dark cobalt blue wrap dress with silver accessories, and strappy wedge sandals for walking around outside. Patty wore a beautiful teal green suit and gold hoop earrings with her hair up in an untidy but very chic bun. Since she'd begun seeing Jack her hair had become looser, messier... Sexier. They checked one last time that the wait staff and helpers were ready for action, and gave each other a quick hug as the first guests began to arrive. Will, Tom, and their parents Jerry and Tanya. Jack, and the select board and bank manager, shop owners and their families, teachers, the doctor and her wife, the coaches and their spouses. Buck. And in the middle of the arrivals, handshakes and well wishes the county Sheriff pulled up and asked for Faith.

Will was standing close by and murmured, "Oh, shit. This is never good." More loudly he said, "Hi Sheriff Grady. What's going on?"

"Will," the sheriff nodded his acknowledgement, "Can you tell me who Faith Nicholas is?"

Faith strode up to him.

"Good afternoon sheriff. How can I help you? Or have you come to join the party?"

"No, ma'am. I need to see your permit for an outdoor function and temporary outdoor liquor license. And I need to see the state serving certificates for all of your bartenders."

Jack and Patty were standing nearby, listening.

45

"Who would have called him on this?" Jack whispered. *"He never shows up unless a complaint is filed."*

"Yes, sir." Faith motioned for the sheriff to follow. Will was close behind, followed by Patty and Jack. They made there way into the inn and to the front desk. Will, Jack and Patty hung back while the sheriff leaned on the counter and Faith disappeared into the office. She returned soon after with three folders.

"Here you are, sheriff. This is the permit for today's party, this is our temporary liquor license to serve outdoors, and these are my workers' state certifications to serve alcohol. I have photos with each of them if you'd like to go outside and check everyone. My mom and I both completed the owner's course and our certificates are in there as well. Anything else that you need?" Faith asked sweetly.

"No, ma'am. I have to say I am pleasantly surprised by your attention to detail here. Most innkeepers never check to see what they need for permits before throwin' a shindig like this. And they never pay attention to maximum occupancy. Good job, young lady."

Faith smiled her best hospitality industry smile. "Are you still officially on duty or can you join us outside for a snack?" His belly was that of a man who liked to eat.

"Well, now. I think I can have a bite while I'm here." The five of them began the walk to the yard.

"You've done this place up nice. I'm gonna remember this next time my mother-in-law's in town."

Faith laughed.

"So Clyde, who blew her in?" asked Jack.

"Jack, you know that's supposed to be confidential."

Faith handed the sheriff a glass of bourbon punch. He took a sip.

"Young lady, this is quite nice. Very smooth. And because you seem like a nice gal and from what I can see you're running a nice place I'll tell you this; you don't have friends at The Overlook Lodge at the ski area."

"Hmm. That's too bad." Faith said sadly.

"That's ridiculous!" Will exclaimed. "They don't do the Inn-to-Inn tours, and they have 100 rooms. They're a hotel, not an inn. What's their problem?"

"Well, I can't say for sure," the sheriff answered, "but part of the problem might be that Kim Edgeworth is the marketing gal up there."

46

Jack coughed and turned away. Will's jaw dropped.

"She's back in town, Will, and found herself a job at The Overlook."

"Who, may I ask, is Kim Edgeworth?" Faith looked between Will and the sheriff.

"Best Will answers that one, m'dear. Those shrimp over there look good..." The sheriff wandered toward the bar.

Faith raised her eyebrows. Will closed his eyes and shook his head. Jack grabbed Patty's hand.

"Let's give them a minute."

Will led Faith to a settee in the great room and sat next to her. He looked nervous. More than nervous, unnerved.

"Kim Edgeworth is my ex."

"So? Everybody has exes..."

"Not like her, they don't. The reason she's my ex is that she is mentally ill. Really. The sheriff actually got involved and I almost had a restraining order taken on her."

"What? Seriously?"

"Yeah. We were actually engaged. Picked a date and everything. She'd been after me to propose as soon as we graduated high school; I'm still not sure why I did. We were so young."

"Did you love her?"

"I dunno, as much as you can love someone at 18. It was one of those things... We'd been high school sweethearts. Everybody just expected we'd get married. I don't even know how I felt. But it was like as soon as she got that ring she turned into a madwoman." Will shook his head.

"Like bridezilla?"

"Bridezilla was a squeaky toy compared to Kim Edgeworth. She was demanding, and compulsive... Starved herself if I didn't agree to something she wanted for the wedding, stalked me on our evenings apart, even came at me with a knife once when I told her I needed some space. She was totally out of control. No one mentioned there was a history of mental illness in the family; she was finally diagnosed with bi-polar disorder, OCD and schizophrenia. Her dad came to me and told me they needed to hospitalize her. I couldn't handle it. I was a kid... that was a long time ago. We were so young. I broke it off with her after she was stabilized. She seemed pretty normal once she was on her meds, but I told her I thought we'd moved too fast. She was

47

so upset I thought they'd have to hospitalize her again. Her folks are good people. They tried to convince her it was for the best, but she wasn't having it. She continued to stalk me. They moved away to get her away from me. I heard they'd moved to Maryland, her dad's family's from there. I haven't seen her since."

"And no one knew she was back?"

"Apparently no one who wanted to tell *me*..."

"Will, we're not even officially a couple... Why would she care about my business?"

"I don't know. Unless the grapevine is saying more than what's true... She knew The Jay Feather belonged to my family; maybe she thinks I'm running it now."

"Well, your truck is outside a lot..." Faith smiled sarcastically.

"It's just all too weird. Please promise me you'll be careful. I don't want anything to happen to you." Will looked serious.

"Point taken. I will. You going to be okay?" Faith asked.

"You know... I don't know." Will closed his eyes and hung his head.

Jack gave Patty the Cliff's Notes version of Will's tale, and as any mother would be Patty was immediately concerned for both Faith and Will.

"Is she dangerous, do you think?" she asked.

"Not if she takes her meds. And I have to think she wouldn't have been hired at The Overlook if they thought she was unbalanced."

"True."

"Lets all just be careful and alert, and hope this is no big deal."

Faith and Will came outside and Patty reached for her daughter, pulling her into a hug.

"We'll get through this," she whispered. "Will," she said, "please be cautious. We don't want anything to happen to you." Patty smiled.

"Thanks, me neither," he wisecracked.

Tom joined them and asked what had happened with the sheriff, as he noticed the sheriff partaking in the festivities. Will pulled Tom aside to explain. Faith could see Tom's eyes open wide and a frightened look cross his face.

48

Before long the word had spread that Kim Edgeworth was back in town. Small towns tend to protect their own, but also love the chance to gossip, so Patty and Faith heard stories from everyone. The theme was the same: mentally ill, unbalanced girl makes life miserable for sweet, naive boy. But what no one could say was how Kim Edgeworth fared *now*. Was she stable? Did she have an agenda? Why was she back?

This excitement couldn't overshadow The Jay Feather's grand opening party, though. People talked and laughed, ate and danced. Pretty much everyone in town showed up and many walked through the inn for the first time since it had opened. Faith kept a couple of rooms available for people to view, and everyone remarked how lovely it all was, and how they looked forward to having their out of town family and guests stay there when their own guestrooms had overflowed. At the end of the day Faith was tired and pleased, and a bit sad as she knew her mother would soon leave for Manhattan.

Patty arrived back at her apartment on the Upper East Side late the next day. She sat on her sofa with a stack of mail and a cup of tea but couldn't focus on the task at hand. She kept thinking about Faith, Will, The Jay Feather, the town of O'Dell, and Jack. She already missed all of them, and was worried about Faith and Will. Would Kim Edgeworth be a problem for them? Patty would have to be in close contact and listen for any sign of upset from Faith, as Faith was really good at trying not to worry her mother. Without seeing Faith's *tell* of the wiggling fingers or the head tilt Patty might not know what was really going on. So she'd better get back up there soon. Soon would also mean seeing Jack. Patty's heart fluttered when she thought of him. Them. Whatever this was it brought her happiness. He was fun, nice, affectionate, *appropriate*. And the sex was great. Patty had a lot to make up for, having been without someone in her life for *years*. She hoped he felt the same, and that he would be able to put up with their distance between visits. She contemplated calling him right then. No, that would be ridiculous, she thought, I just said goodbye this morning. And what a fabulous goodbye it had been.

She'd stayed at Jack's last night. He said he wanted to spend the night with his arms around her to have that muscle memory until she came back to town. Only a coach would use "muscle memory" amorously, she told him. They kissed and talked and made sweet love before sleep, wound around each other in the cool of his bedroom. In the morning he plied her with soft kisses and caresses, and before she was fully awake she was aching for him, crazy with lust in her dreams. He was ready for her. She rolled on top of him, sliding onto him, her hair wild and unfettered. He whispered how gorgeous she was, how hot she made him, and she rode him fiercely until her spasms of release overtook her. He climaxed soon after and they lay happily exhausted in each other's arms. Later he brought her coffee in bed, and she confessed how she would miss him when she left. He smiled sheepishly.

"You have no idea how much I'll miss *you*," he said.

Jack drove Patty to the inn that morning to pack up her things and say her goodbyes. After a long hug from Faith during which they promised regular calls to check-in, Jack drove Patty to the train. Having to kiss her goodbye was torture.

"I'll be back soon," she promised. "You'll get busy with stuff and forget I was ever here," she joked.

"Nope. I'm not going to change the sheets so I can smell your perfume on the pillow."

"Ewww! After what we did in those sheets?" she whispered.

Just thinking of the day made her miss him. And truth be told, a little horny. Her phone rang; it was Jack.

"I was just thinking about you," she answered.

"Good. Say, listen. How do you feel about phone sex?"

Will spent a sleepless night thinking about Kim Edgeworth. He called the inn in the morning and left a message for Faith that he'd be out this morning and that he'd start work after noon sometime. And then he drove to The Overlook.

The Overlook Lodge was located about forty minutes from O'Dell, at the Green Mountain Ski Area. It was the biggest of the hotels and nearest the slopes, with 100 rooms and a fine dining restaurant. It attracted visitors from all over the world, and held conferences and weddings in the off-season, making it a year-round destination. It was also part of the property Jack Kimball's family had sold, making him and his parents comfortable for life. The post and beam

50

construction made the hotel look like an oversized high-end log cabin, with huge windows providing views of both the ski area and valley below. Will went to the front desk and asked for Kim Edgeworth. He realized his hands were shaking. The clerk called her office and directed Will to a chair by the fireplace to wait. He didn't wait long. Kim Edgeworth strode quickly through the lobby, and before Will had even fully stood up threw herself into his arms.

"Will! It's so great to see you! I'm so glad you came!" She kissed him full on the lips.

"Whoa, Kim. Hold up." He grasped her arms and held her away from him. She looked puzzled.

"What's wrong? You don't want to kiss me?" She smiled seductively.

"Kim, we haven't seen each other in what, twelve years? A lot has changed..."

"Really, Will? Of course it has. I'm better, you know, so stop worrying. I didn't come back to stalk you. I take my meds like a good girl. I'm here because my company sent me here."

Will let her go, and she motioned for him to sit on the sofa. She sat in the adjacent chair.

"What company is that?" he asked.

"CLI Hotel Group. Had you heard The Overlook changed hands last year?"

"Yeah, I had, some foreign investors or something. I never heard a name."

"They're privately held, so they keep everything pretty close to the vest. I've been working for them since I got out of college."

Will looked surprised, considering what a mess Kim was the last time he saw her. Kim rolled her eyes.

"Yes, Will. I went to college. University of Maryland. They have a great business school. I majored in marketing and minored in finance. CLI picked me up out of school and I've been with them in hotels all over the world. I almost said no to this gig. I was afraid of coming back here, but I guess I can't hide forever. I really am OK."

"I'm glad to hear it, Kim. I really am. But I have to ask a question." He paused. "I was at a party in town yesterday, at the inn. Did you know my folks sold the inn and it's open for business again?"

She nodded, grinning, like she knew what was coming.

"It was nothing against the new owner, Will. I look around at competition in the area and if there's anything interesting going on I always nudge the authorities to make sure they're pulling their permits and that everything is above board."

"That's pretty shameless. Do other hotels do that to you?"

"No. It's just my way of keeping ahead of the curve. It gives me an idea of who is on top of their game, so when its time for acquisitions I know who to go after first. This stuff is all a matter of public record."

"The Jay Feather isn't for sale, Kim. It just opened. It's been Faith's lifelong dream to have a place like this." Will could feel the heat rise in his face, but he'd managed to keep his voice down.

"Wow, you're pretty worked up over this, Will. Do you have a *relationship* with this woman?"

"What's it to you if I do? Look Kim, just keep your distance."

"Or what?" She looked bored.

Will glared at her, and without a word he stormed out. Kim watched him go with a smile playing at her mouth.

Will hadn't told Faith of his meeting with Kim, but Faith could sense what seemed to be a sense of unease in Will. She wanted to ask him about it but the inn was busy so she never got the chance. Patty was checking in regularly and was happy to hear there was nothing to report. Jack would swing by for a drink to make sure all was well, and even Tom checked in with Faith more than usual. She thought it was so he could see Iris, but he came in for a cup of tea even when Iris's car wasn't in the lot. She felt protected and at ease, and having a big Jamaican in the kitchen also helped.

Rita came into the office about a week later with a beautiful bouquet of fall colored flowers; orange gerbera daisies, yellow and white Montauks, sunflowers, wheat sprigs and salmon colored roses.

"Wow! Who are they from?" Faith asked.

"The card is sealed," Rita said, "I left it for you."

Congratulations on your new business. I'd love to have lunch some day. Please call me at your convenience.

52

Kimberly Edgeworth
Marketing Director,
The Overlook Hotel, a CLI Hotel Property
"Hmm. I don't know whether to laugh or buy a gun."

Kim left her office later than she expected and it was long past dark when she pulled in to the driveway of her rented cottage. She hadn't left a light on and she took some time fumbling with her keys in the darkness. She didn't hear him come up behind her. She gasped as he put his arms around her and began to kiss her neck.

"You knew I'd come," he whispered. He sucked on her earlobe and moved his hands up to her breasts. She didn't stop him. He turned her head and stuck his tongue in her mouth. She moaned as he pinched her nipples. She managed to break free enough to get the door open and he pushed her inside. He pushed her to the sofa and lifted her skirt. It took him no time to pull her panties off. He quickly freed his manhood and entered her from behind. She gasped again and again every time he slammed into her.

"Do you remember this? Huh? Do you remember how good this was?" he asked, panting. He was banging at her fiercely, and she arched her back as she began her climax.

"Oh, yeah, baby. That's it, come on," he whispered as he began to lose control. He moaned his pleasure as he continued to thrust, and then finally slowed, slumping over her, spent.

Faith never told anyone Kim had sent flowers. She always had fresh flowers in the foyer, so these were not conspicuous in their presence. She mulled it over for a few days and came to the conclusion that the adage *keep your friends close and your enemies closer* was probably wise. She called Kim Edgeworth and made a lunch date; Faith invited her to see the inn.

Neither Iris or Delroy was happy when they found out Kim was coming to the inn, so even though they didn't work at lunchtime, they told Faith they'd be there to serve and cook. She was happy her staff was so concerned and supportive, and she welcomed the help. They'd also agreed not to tell Will what was going on.

"Boss lady, I put some scotch bonnet in her soup. You never see her again."

Faith laughed.

"No, Delroy. Just serve the lunch we planned. But I appreciate the thought."

They would be lunching on curried squash soup, roasted pear and beet salad over arugula with toasted walnuts, sunflower seeds and shallot vinaigrette, freshly baked French bread and a caramelized apple tart. The table nearest the windows was set with white linen, and Faith had used a few of the flowers from Kim's bouquet in a low arrangement for the table.

Faith was ready. She was casually dressed in cream slacks, black suede boots, a black turtleneck sweater and bold silver jewelry. Her hair was long and loose. Delroy was very complementary.

"Ya mon, you make that look g-o-o-o-d."

He was putting a dish of spiced pecans on the table. Hank had followed him out of the kitchen. The dog usually went between the kitchen and the barn but didn't usually come into the common areas unless Will was around. Faith looked around nervously, thinking maybe Will was nearby, but there was no sight of him. Strange, she thought. When Delroy went back into the kitchen Hank stayed by her side.

Kimberly Edgewood drove the long drive and pulled up outside of The Jay Feather Inn right on time. She was impressed. The renovations and landscaping made the place look much different than she remembered it when she was a teenager spending time in her boyfriend's house. It was a bit strange to be there, and she felt a little shaky. She took a deep breath and ticked off her checklist in her head. Yes, she'd turned off the iron, and washed her hands, twice. Even after the meds the obsessive-compulsive disorder could still be a problem. She smiled her brightest smile and opened the front door.

Faith looked up to see a fashionable woman walk into the inn. She had a chin length light brown bob, big brown eyes and wore a Chanel-style copper suit with black trim and black pumps. As she turned to look at Faith she smiled, and Hank began a low growl. Faith looked down at him.

"Seriously, Hank? Perhaps you'd better get back into the kitchen." The Akita looked up at her, blinked and headed out. Did Hank know something she didn't? Faith approached her guest.

"Kimberly? I'm Faith Nicholas." She offered her hand. Kim shook it warmly.

"I'm so glad to meet you! Please, call me Kim."

"Of course. Come in. Would you like a tour?"

"Yes, great!"

Faith showed Kim the unoccupied guest rooms, pointed out the renovated areas, and then walked through the common areas and the bar. They finally entered the dining room and sat at the beautifully laid table.

"So who is doing your renovation work?" Kim asked.

"Will Grant," she replied, openly and brightly, "He's very good."

"Hmm, yes, I know," Kim cooed. "We were engaged, you know."

"Yes, actually I did know." Faith's face was smiling and serene, and Kim wasn't sure whether Faith knew all the details of her past. Or not.

"He came to see me recently! Did he tell you?" Kim licked her lips suggestively.

Faith was not expecting *that*, but she kept her poker face.

"That's so nice! He's such a good guy." She didn't answer Kim's question.

"Yes, I'm sure he and I will be seeing more of each other."

Faith continued to smile blithely, but couldn't help but feel, what? Jealous?

"So, Kim, was there anything special you wanted to discuss while we're together? Or was this just a networking opportunity?"

Iris had served the soup and bread, and the two women began to eat. Iris had offered wine, but both declined.

"Actually, I just really wanted to see what you'd done with the place. I'd spent so much time here when I was young. I used to help Tanya with Thanksgiving dinner, and we had such great Christmas parties. It feels good to be home!"

This is not your home, bitch, Faith thought.

"Will told me this had been a lifelong dream of yours, to open an inn." Kim added.

Now Faith was feeling at a bit of a disadvantage. What else did she know?

"Yes, I've been in hospitality for a long time but really wanted to be able to settle in one place and truly establish a business. The moving around does get old."

"Oh, I've liked the travel. My company has moved me around quite a bit and when I'm between projects they send me to shop for properties. I've been to 17 countries in the last six years."

Faith thought now Kim was just showing off.

"How long is your project at The Overlook?"

"Not sure yet. Our CEO is coming to take a look around the area sometime in the next couple of months, and he'll decide if I'm to stay or go."

Too bad it's not sooner, Faith thought. Iris brought out the salads and offered fresh ground pepper.

"Are you doing the cooking?" Kim asked.

"These are my recipes."

"But you have help?"

"Are you trying to poach my sous chef?" Faith asked, smiling.

"I'm always on the lookout for fresh talent... But don't worry, we don't have any openings right now."

Delroy and Iris were listening from the kitchen door.

"Mos def not gonna work for dat scrawny white bitch," Delroy whispered. Iris had to suppress a giggle. The kitchen door opened and Hank trotted in, followed by Will. Delroy jumped into action.

"Respect, mon! It's lunch time, you need some grub? Sit right here at de counter, I take care of you, mon."

"I was looking for Faith. Hank was acting all strange out in the barn. Making that howling noise he makes when we get close to the inn, but we're already here. It's weird. I just thought I'd check on her."

"She's in a meeting with another hospitality person." Iris's eyes were wide. She didn't lie, but she didn't tell the whole truth. In the meantime Hank nosed his way into the dining room and started the low growl again. Will pushed by Iris and followed him in. When he saw Faith and Kim having lunch his heart almost stopped. He commanded Hank back into the kitchen and strode purposefully to the table.

"Kim. What are you doing here?"

"Hi Will!" She grabbed his hand. "I was just coming to see what our old place looked like!"

Will pulled his hand away.

"So you've seen it. Now go."

"Will, honey. Don't be rude!" Kim chided.

"What do you want?" He was terse.

Faith watched like it was a tennis match.

"So far I think it was to make me uncomfortable, to check out my business, and to try to poach my sous chef." Faith ticked off on her fingers. "She failed on two counts, and I'm not sure she really cares about my business." Will had laid his hand on Faith's shoulder, and when she reached up and grabbed his hand he didn't pull it away. He brought it to his lips and kissed it. Kim's face darkened.

"Don't be so sure I don't care about your business," Kim snapped. "If CLI wants this place you'll never be able to stop us getting it."

Faith laughed.

"Why would a big operation like CLI want The Jay Feather? And since I'm the sole proprietor if I don't want to sell it I don't have to!"

Kim stood up.

"Don't be so sure, Faith Nicholas. I've seen it done. And you don't own the place, the bank does. And guess who owns the bank?"

Faith was shaken when Kim Edgeworth left the inn. She could deal with confrontation but she didn't like it much. Will grabbed her and held her.

"I'm sorry you had to go through that," he said

"Why didn't you tell me you'd seen her?" She pulled back to look at him. He looked away.

"Why didn't you tell me she was coming for lunch?" His eyebrows rose.

"I thought I could handle it," she said, looking down. "Look at us. Trying to protect each other. I guess we need to work on our communication skills."

"Yeah, I guess." Will seemed evasive.

"I think we need to talk about the implications of her last statement. My mom's coming for the weekend. It'll be good to bounce this off of her."

"Jack might be a good resource, too," he added.

"Thanks. I know this is all really weird but thanks for trying to come to the rescue. I would probably have gotten her to say what she wanted, though. It just would have taken me longer."

"Sorry. It's your business and I should trust you to run it, but she scares me. And I, well, I... I just want to take care of you. I... I know I said I wouldn't do this but..." He leaned in and kissed her. She kissed him back.

Iris and Delroy stood in the doorway and high fived each other.

SIX

Ciaran Lynch's offices were on the top floor of one of London's most expensive properties, with expansive views of the Thames. The boardroom where he now presided over his weekly scheduled business review seated twenty, but today only six of his direct reports joined him at the table. Ciaran Lynch International, or CLI, owned hotels, inns, resorts and time-share properties internationally, but they weren't in the business of planning and building these properties; they sought out successful businesses and bought them out. Lynch's philosophy was that a successful property could be purchased for less than the money it took to build one, especially if you took into account the revenue loss during building, furnishing, training staff, and marketing when no rooms were being sold. Upgrading was easier and took less time. Good staff would be asked to stay. And some of the stately buildings that made up the company's portfolio could never be reproduced.

The U.S. proved an interesting challenge for CLI. They of course owned some of the old art deco hotels in Miami's South Beach, two boutique properties in New York City, a beautiful resort in Hawaii and a smattering of newer hotels in the major airline hubs across the country. But they had only one property in New England, The Overlook Hotel in Green Mountain, VT. Today's meeting was to review potential larger hotel opportunities in Boston, Providence, and Portland, and to discuss which strategy to take in the rest of New England. Randy Preston, the VP for the Eastern U.S. was laying out his findings.

"Ciaran, here's how I see the New England situation. People going skiing that are looking for an upscale experience aren't staying at the Marriot Courtyard. They're staying at swanky inns and small B&Bs where they serve local craft beer and local organic food. There are a few chef owned locations that have a year round clientele from skiers, hiker and bikers, and they cater weddings and farm to table dinners. Because these guys are small there isn't a lot of industry data, but from the intel we've gathered if they do enough weddings they don't care if it snows or not; they're set for the year. So the key is to keep the charm of the small inn but provide the buying efficiencies we can leverage by owning multiple properties. This could cover food and beverage costs as well as linens and even some utilities. We can also share resources like kitchen staff, catering staff, and, if the properties are close enough, even chambermaids." Randy, while based in New York, was originally from Vermont and had worked the ski area hotels and inns in college.

"So, you're tellin' me we should be spendin' the money on the wee places and run them like they were a chain?" Ciaran's brogue had diminished over his years of international travel but was evident when he was tired, as he was now.

"Not identical units, that's not what people want. Keep the charm of the individual places but let them benefit from the economies of scale we can provide. I think if we can saturate an area with our brand we can actually create a demand. These ski areas suffer from skiers waiting until close to the weekend to see what the weather and the conditions will be like. They used to book months in advance, but with today's technology they wait until the last minute. If we have, say, ten properties that service a central ski area we could create the demand. Concerts with big name artists, conferences, circuit cup races…"

"You may be on to somethin' lad." Lynch put his fist to his chin, deep in thought. "Have you got any properties lined up to give a look?"

"We do," Randy replied, "our marketing director at The Overlook Hotel is on it. I know your schedule has you in the states next month. I can have a list put together to review in New York while you're there."

"I hear New England is lovely this time of year. If we're to be spendin' me money there I'd bloody well like to see the place."

SEVEN

Ciaran Lynch was tired because he worked too much. He'd recently returned from his outposts in Singapore and Bali, was jet lagged and fairly cranky. His wife Marthe was on holiday and his sixteen-year-old son Brendan was away at school, so neither was at home when he arrived. Even with the housekeeper and his driver around the place felt empty. Not that it felt much different when his family was home. Brendan was at an age that his friends, social media and electronics were far more important that his parents, and Marthe, a successful silkscreen artist, was either working or at an opening for her own work or that of a colleague's. Ciaran didn't begrudge her this life as he worked so much himself. Marthe seemed happy and was well suited to being the wife of a world travelling businessman. She enjoyed the solitude and the time to focus on her work, and when they were together they enjoyed each other, both physically and emotionally. The sex was great, Marthe was funny and engaging, and didn't expect to be entertained. He felt himself a lucky man.

Ciaran's rise in the hospitality industry was well planned. He watched his parents struggle and as a teenager knew there had to be a better way. His father told him it was the lot of the Irish to be the serving class, but Ciaran didn't believe it. He knew the way to a better life was through a good education, including his MBA. After working in the hospitality industry throughout university he went on to worm his way, with the help of his smoldering, Black Irish good looks, into jobs at the places deemed the highest ranked by travel writers for their service and hospitality, including stints at a tented safari camp in Kenya, the best hotels in Europe and ski areas in Switzerland. He even worked at a base camp for rich mountain climbers in the Himalayas. During this time he scrimped and saved money, and invested in a new computer company called Apple. Eventually he invested in additional tech stocks, and with his business intuition sensed a change was coming. He got out of the rest of these investments right before the .com bubble burst. He became a relatively wealthy man. He began buying hotels and transformed them into the high service, high ratio of staff to client oases they now were. And he continued his rise.

Ciaran realized the middle class weren't travelling during this economic downturn, but they weren't his clientele anyway. The rich were, and they still had money. So his business plan worked. Buy hotels in the right spots, make them into high-end luxury places of respite for the wealthy, make money, and do it again.

He hired the best people, straight from school so he could make them into the service-oriented staff his hotels needed, or poached them from other hotels that were silly enough to post their *employees of the month* in the lobbies. His workforce was strong, loyal, and silent. Invisible to their guests until something was required, and then satisfying this need usually before the guest even realized they required it.

Ciaran Lynch was wealthy, happy with his family, and as successful as he could have imagined. But something was missing. He had offered his parents an easy retirement anywhere in the world they'd like to go, but they wouldn't give up their pub in County Cork. For as hard as they worked they would never give up their town, their friends, their customers... their lifestyle. Ciaran was rich and he would never have to slave to make a living as his parents had, but he had no connection to his work, and no community. He had some acquaintances with whom he played squash, a few husbands of Marthe's friends he'd make small talk with at art openings, but no real, true friends. He'd never slowed down enough to nurture any friendships, and he was starting to realize his ambition had taken its toll.

Thinking about this made him uncomfortable, and he'd spent his entire life trying to become comfortable, so arriving at the place to which he aspired and finding himself still unhappy was disconcerting. He searched his soul for what might be the answer. What did he really want? He realized he didn't know.

EIGHT

Patty, Jack and Faith met over the weekend during a lull in the inn's daily routine. Guests were out hiking, biking, or shopping, and those who chose to do nothing at the inn were sitting in rocking chairs on the porch enjoying the beautiful autumn weather. Faith had Rita lay out woven throws on the backs of the chairs every morning in case the weather got cool, and many of Faith's customers were presently snuggled beneath them. The hot, spiced apple cider in the lobby and the apple cider caramels made for contented guests. The inn was quiet and Faith knew she'd have some time for this meeting before they came in for cocktails and dinner. The library was tucked away from the main lobby. It was a great place for a gathering that needed to be out of earshot, and it was cozy; the fire in the hearth took the chill out of the place.

Faith sipped her tea and recounted the confrontation she and Will had with Kim Edgeworth. When she finished she looked at them and exhaled audibly.

"I don't know what to think," she said. "I don't know if they can change the terms of the mortgage agreement."

"I'd ask your lawyers to look at the fine print to see if there is any possible way the bank can call the loan," Jack suggested.

"They're already on it. I Fed-Ex'd them a copy earlier this week," she replied.

"Even if they can call the note, Sweetie, we can come up with the funds to pay it if we have to," Patty added. "I know you need operating funds until the inn turns a profit, so you shouldn't touch the rest of your inheritance, but I can cash in some investments..."

"No, mom. I don't want to touch your investments. You've worked hard for that money and I was hoping you'd retire early to enjoy some of it!" Faith was almost in tears. "It could be a long time before I'd be able to pay it all back. Maybe a new loan from a different lender?" Faith mused.

"Possibly, but that could take time," Jack offered. "Faith, I've done OK with my investments and I could offer up a loan. Perhaps between your mother and I we could cover the current loan. If the bank is out of the picture there is no way anyone can take this away from you."

"Jack, you hardly know us!" Faith whispered, even though she was pretty sure her mom knew Jack pretty well at this point.

"I'd like to change that," Jack smiled, looking at Patty. Patty blushed. Faith looked back and forth between them and smiled.

"So if the lawyers say we have a problem then we can say we have a potential solution?" she asked.

Patty and Jack nodded, still looking at each other, smiling.

Will went home to lock up Roots and Sky before heading back to the inn to have dinner with Jack, Tom, and his parents, who were in town for the weekend. After saying goodnight to the farmer's market crew he grabbed an apple from the basket marked *macouns* and started munching as he and Hank made their way to the back door of the farmhouse. Will saw an unfamiliar car in the driveway and Hank started to growl. Will opened the back door and Hank bound into the kitchen, still growling.

"Hank, heel," Will commanded. He wasn't sure who was in the house but he didn't want Hank to take them down unless it was necessary. He cautiously walked into the den, with Hank close on his heels. Kim was sitting comfortably on the sofa, legs crossed seductively, clad in one of Will's flannel shirts and not much else.

"What are you doing here Kim?" Will asked, as Hank continued to growl.

"What does it look like, Will? Waiting for you of course," she purred.

"Kim, get your clothes and get out."

"Why? You can't deny how good we are together," she cooed seductively.

"Kim, you can't be here."

"What do you mean?"

"My parents have an apartment here, and Tom lives with me. And actually, I expect all of them home very soon, so you need to get your clothes on..."

"You're just saying that," she smiled. "Come sit by me and I'll show you how much I want you." She patted the sofa cushion next to her.

Will wasn't sure what to do. If he left she might stay and embarrass Tom and maybe his parents. Maybe even vandalize his house. If he stayed he might have to call the sheriff to remove her. What might she do then?

"Will, you ready?" Jack called from the kitchen as he walked toward the den. He turned the corner and saw Kim on the couch in just a flannel shirt. "Kim? What are you doing?" He looked back and forth between Kim and Will, trying to figure out what was going on.

"You were interrupting us Jack. We were just about to..." Will cut her off.

"Kim was just leaving," Will said.

Kim assessed the situation. She decided the best way to play this was to leave, since Will obviously had plans. Kim got dangerously close to Will as she walked past him, and then walked up the stairs to retrieve her clothes from Will's room.

"Thanks, Jack," Will said quietly. Jack wasn't sure what to think. Had she been here with Will all afternoon?

"Delroy told me her car was here when we passed each other in the inn parking lot. He recognized it from last week. So I thought I'd swing in to see if everything was OK."

Kim breezed past the two men and growling dog. She turned at the door and looked at Will.

"Soon, darling." She blew him a seductive kiss, then left.

Will just stared after her.

NINE

Faith knew when she came to the inn that if she wasn't careful the stress of a new business and the amount of work she'd have to do would take it's toll on her. So she had started a workout routine when she first came to O'Dell and was religious about sticking to it. Every morning while the inn was quiet she'd come into the common area and start the coffee prep. Regular, decaf, and water for tea and hot chocolate were always available to inn guests, so she'd put on the first pot before she left the inn for her run. Delroy was always grateful to have coffee ready when he arrived to start breakfast, and Rita would brew the rest when she came in.

There was a loop Faith could run quickly, it was about 4 miles and the first half was all uphill, so it took her about 35 minutes to complete her run. The first day that she ran her lungs rebelled against the uphill climb, and her calves and thighs rebelled against the downhill stretch. Now all her body parts were cooperating and she was able to go at a good pace and not feel like she was going to die the next day, but that hill was still a killer.

Her run took her south for a bit and then turned east and up the mountain, passing some homesteads on the right and the logging trail cut in back of her property. Eventually her path turned north into the beautiful wilderness of the mountain where nothing but the sounds of the birds could be heard and the trees created a canopy over the road. This stretch connected back to the main road and the bike path leading back into town, a safe paved road for Faith's last sprint before making her way into the inn for coffee and a shower.

Today she really needed this run. The possible mortgage issues, and Kim Edgeworth, weighed heavily on her. Jack had told Patty about Kim showing up at Will's house. Patty of course told Faith, and Faith wasn't sure what to think. Was Will interested in Kim? Was he already rekindling a relationship with his ex? Or was Kim really crazy? Faith thought she and Will were becoming closer all the time, but they still hadn't consummated their relationship. Will continued to tell Faith that it was fine, that they had time and he didn't want to rush her. But Faith felt guilty for keeping him waiting. Her focus really had to be the inn. But many nights as she was closing the bar Will would just swing by to say goodnight. She'd walk to the truck with him, and they would proceed to make out like teenagers while sitting on his tailgate. Thankfully he'd park by the barn where no one could see them.

He'd hop up on the truck bed and pat the tailgate next to him, looking at her with bedroom eyes. Hank would raise his head from his slumber in the truck, and when he saw who it was would heave a heavy sigh and go back to sleep. Faith would boost herself up next to Will, and they'd talk for a bit. Somehow he always managed to get her to lean her head on his shoulder, and the next thing she knew they had their arms around each other. His soft, sweet kisses would start on her hairline while they talked, then move down to the bridge of her nose, then her eyelids. When he found her lips she was ready, wanting him in the worst way. He'd be gentle at first; slow, easy kisses, a nibble on her lip or her chin, then more persistent. A long, slow, wet kiss, his tongue probing hers and getting the response he wanted, their mouths locked and their heartbeats racing. He'd pull her back into the truck bed, and they would kiss and fondle each other until they thought they couldn't stand it. Will would look at her and smile.

"Someday, woman, you are going to be all mine. *All* mine."

"And I promise it will have been worth the wait," Faith would say as she smiled back, kissed him one last time and sauntered back to the inn. But was putting him off pushing him back to Kim? Was she teasing him? Did she need to stop? Would she push him into Kim's arms for sure if she did? Or maybe it was time. Maybe she could manage a relationship and her business. She was kind of doing that already. This was one more thing she really didn't want to have to think about today.

Faith had never had a true long-term relationship. She certainly had never met the right guy, but even the ones she was comfortable with she never felt she had time for. She was driven: driven to buy her own business and driven to have a permanent home. But to what end if there was no one to share it with? Her grandparents seemed to have a good relationship, but she didn't know for sure. It would have been easy to hide their true feelings from their only grandchild who felt like the center of the universe when she was with them. And her mom certainly wasn't a role model for relationships. A role model for a driven career woman? Certainly. For a significant other? Not so much. Faith always wondered what her mom's life would have been like if she hadn't had a baby at eighteen. Probably easier. Faith knew she herself had accomplished a lot in her young life, possibly because she was unencumbered with a spouse and/or a child. Perhaps being solitary made the most sense. So why did it feel so good to kiss Will and think about what their future might be?

She needed to focus on business. She was expecting to hear from her lawyer soon about the mortgage, and hoping for good news. But what if it wasn't? Should she take loans from Jack and her mom?

She'd never encountered anyone on her run before, other than an occasional passing car. It was early. She'd see a light on in a window, smoke swirling from a chimney now that the weather was cooler, but never anyone outside, so she was surprised when she saw an old man sitting on a tree stump by his driveway. He was watching her with interest.

"Are you the young lady that owns The Jay Feather Inn?" he asked.

"Yes, sir," she huffed. "My name's Faith." She stood with her hands on her knees to catch her breath, reaching her right hand out to shake the one he offered.

"Glad to know ya. I've been expecting ya," he said.

"Really?" she asked.

"This guy lets me know you're a comin'." He pointed to the tree next to his shed, where a big blue jay was perched, looking at them. Faith's eyes filled with tears as she thought of her grandfather.

"How?" she asked the old gent.

"He squawks like a crazy bird every morning, and as soon as he stops you run by. He knows you're on your way, young lady. And he's here to see you every day."

"Thank you for telling me," she sniffed back her tears.

"Did you lose someone you love?" he asked. Faith looked surprised.

"My grandfather. How did you know?"

"The big birds, the jays and the cardinals, and sometimes the robins, they are our lost loved ones in living form. You can feel them around you if you pay attention. That cardinal, there?" he pointed to the pine tree by his back door, "that's my missus. She died in 2010, but she comes to see me every day."

Faith smiled at the thought. How wonderful it would feel to know her grandfather was close by.

"What's your name?" she asked him.

"Gus. Gus Norman," he replied, shaking her hand again. "That blue jay, he waits every day for you. Like he's checking to make sure you're OK. That's what I think."

"I wish he could talk to me, and tell me what to do," Faith said softly.

"I think you know what to do," he said looking into her eyes. "You just have to trust it's the right thing."

Faith almost laughed. It was exactly what her grandfather would have said to her.

"Gus, will you come to the inn to have coffee with me sometime?" she asked.

"You don't want an old coot like me around with all you young 'uns."

"I'd love to talk to you. I miss my grandpa a lot and you are a lot like him. It would be my pleasure to have you visit me."

"Well then, I may just meander down sometime. You got anything stronger than coffee down there? My missus made me promise I'd not keep any in the house, but I do like a nice whiskey every now and again."

"We sure do, Gus. Any time you want." Faith gave the old gent a kiss on his bearded cheek. "See you soon."

Gus waved to her as she ran off. He looked up at the blue jay.

"Nice granddaughter you've got there, my friend." The bird squawked.

TEN

Iris was hard at work on her potting wheel. Her clothes were caked with clay and she had a bandana over her crazy hair. It was her day off, so her focus had been on getting some new pots thrown before the O'Dell Christmas Festival. Her booth there last year represented about fifty percent of her annual pottery sales, so she couldn't afford to get caught without enough inventory. She'd probably never make her entire living from her pottery, but she loved it and it gave her enough money along with her job at the inn to keep a nice apartment and this shared studio space, and to travel once a year to somewhere fun. Her work was in gift shops in several Vermont cities and towns, and Faith had some on display at the inn with Iris's business cards. She did some mail order through her website as well. Maybe someday she'd design a line of pottery that would make her famous, but until then she'd be happy with the status quo. All except for the male companionship part. She loved O'Dell, and didn't want to live anywhere else, but the place wasn't overrun with great prospects. She could sign up with an on-line dating service, but she'd probably only meet guys from Burlington or Rutland, and that was too far away for any kind of relationship. Plus her hours were kind of crazy. Some of the nights she worked at the inn she was there until closing, and it could be 2 AM before she got home. Not a schedule conducive to dating. Pretty good for making pottery, though.

She thought about Tom. A lot. She knew he'd always had a crush on her, and he was nervous around her. He was very intense when he was focused on his work. He had that Vermont mountain man look, the rugged build, curly dark hair that framed his handsome face and dark eyes. And he had the most adorable dimple in his chin. He was usually in a flannel shirt, or a local beer company's tee shirt in the summer, with jeans and work boots. And he smelled of Irish Spring soap. She'd tried to talk to him at work, when he was doing the landscaping at the inn. He spoke easily of the plants and his plans for the flowerbeds, but whenever something personal came up he was tongue-tied. It could be a lot of work to have a relationship with someone like him. Did the Asperger's have anything to do with his difficulties with communication? It must, she guessed. Should she make the

70

first move and try to get to know him better? Would his Asperger's be a stigma that would be hard to live with? Iris wasn't one to care what other people thought, but she'd never been in a relationship with someone that others might try to categorize, or might see as different. And she wasn't sure if she could handle it. If she couldn't she would surely break his heart.

There was a knock on her studio door. When Iris looked up Dan Churchill had stuck his head into the room and was looking around.

"Hi, Dan. Over here," she waved. He spotted her and smiled.

"Hi Iris, hard at work I see."

"Yeah, trying to get some stuff made for the festival," she replied.

"Which is exactly why I'm here." He strode over with a rolled up document that looked like a blueprint. Iris got up, cleaned off her hands and motioned to a worktable.

"You want a cup of tea?" she asked.

"Sure!"

She plugged in her electric kettle and prepped the cups with tea bags. Dan rolled out his plans and used Iris's scissors, matte knife, and tape dispenser to hold down three corners.

"Here's the layout for this year. Santa's house will be here, and Roots and Sky will have this section."

"That's new…" Iris mused.

"Yup, Tom's gonna sell poinsettias, wreaths and some cut trees at the festival this year as well as back at the farm. And the farmer's market is going to have some local cheese, cider, and maple syrup for sale, as well as some root vegetables."

"Wow. This is getting big."

"Yes it is. And I'm here for two reasons. Faith wanted your opinion about The Jay Feather ad for the color brochure, and I want you to pick your booth." Dan offered her the mock up of the brochure. She took a long look at the beautiful ad. It had a winter picture of the inn, surely something Jerry and Tanya Grant had given to Faith, with the website and phone number. The text said "Visit us for lunch at the O'Dell Christmas Festival, right next to Iris Parson Pottery". Iris laughed out loud.

"She makes it sound like I'm a famous potter and people will be flocking to my booth."

"She told me to tell you 'Fake it 'til you make it'." Dan smiled.

"Sounds like Faith," Iris laughed.

"She also had a brainstorm today and wanted me to run it by you."

Iris raised her eyebrows. Dan continued.

"She wanted to know if you could knock out a bunch of soup bowls. She had this idea that the two of you could raise money for charity by selling the soup bowls filled with soup for a premium price with any profit going to charity. People get lunch and they get to take one of your bowls home as well. The Children's Refuge in Burlington is our charity tie-in this year. Any interest?"

"I'll have to think about how. I love the idea but its going to be tough just making enough stock to sell by then. My kiln is pretty small."

"I thought of that. Do you know Booker Pottery in White River Junction?"

"The big commercial place? Sure."

"The owner's son is a buddy of mine. He said we could use the kiln on weekends when they're not in production. The thing is massive."

"I could do everything in one weekend..."

"Yup. So think about it and let me know. Now, you know Faith wants her booth next to yours, so where's it going to be?" Dan asked.

"She's giving me free advertizing in her obviously very expensive ad. She should pick where we are," Iris said, pouring water into the mugs.

"She said you'd say that. She said to tell you this is her first year and you've done this for awhile, so you'd know the best spots." Dan flattened out the plans as Iris handed him his tea.

"Well the best place to be would be here," she pointed to the spots between Roots and Sky and Santa's House, "but that's prime real estate and I don't know if either of us can afford it..."

"I'll make you a deal. If you do the soup bowls for charity I'll charge you the lower rate for those spots. Both you and Faith."

"Deal." Iris shook Dan's hand.

ELEVEN

Brendan Lynch was bored. He was clearly the brightest kid in class, had completed his work and was tutoring others in math and science and doing nothing in study hall but reading John Green books and trying not to laugh too loud. A school break was coming in October so he'd see his Mum for the week, but then there'd be the slog 'til Christmas. His Mum had been on holiday with her friends so he knew they'd just be around home for the break, and that bored him, too. His Da was gone so much he didn't expect to see him this time. In fact he was pretty sure his father didn't even know he had a break coming at all. So Brendan was completely blindsided when his father called him just before tea that night.

"Da? What's wrong? Is Mum alright?"

"Jaysus, Brendan, can't your father ring you up without there being a bloody emergency?"

Brendan laughed. "Sorry, it's just that… Well, you never do!"

"Touché, lad. Your Mum and I were talking. We got a call from the headmaster…"

"Shite," Brendan muttered under his breath.

"Language, lad. Calm yourself, it's nothin' bad."

Brendan relaxed a bit. "What did he say?"

"That you're bored out of your skull. You're way ahead of everyone else in class and you've completed the work through Christmas. He wasn't sure if he should move you to the next level this far into the year, as you'll already have missed the basics in the new classes."

"What did you tell him?"

"That I had a better idea. But I'm asking you, not telling you. You get to decide."

Brendan held his breath again. "What is it?"

"How'd you like to come with me and your mum to the states for awhile?"

"Um… And do what?"

"I have some business in New England. You could look at colleges in Boston, meet up with me in Vermont." Ciaran chuckled. "Not sure exactly, but since I'm going to be there for a while and we haven't spent any time together I thought it might be good. I don't want you turning into a rebellious teenager and torching the library or something."

Brendan laughed. "Yuh, as if."

Ciaran knew he had a good boy, a great kid who was turning into a man, and wanted some time with him before Brendan was totally lost to girls and college.

"So, what do you say?" Now Ciaran was holding his breath.

"Da... This is weird. But OK. I'll go." Brendan didn't let on, but he was excited. He wiggled his fingers and tilted his head.

"Don't sound so excited," Ciaran joked, his own fingers wiggling against his leg.

TWELVE

The next time Iris saw Faith she grabbed her into a hug and thanked her for the free press in the O'Dell Christmas Festival brochure.

"You didn't have to do that, you know." Iris said.

"I know. But you've been a huge help here and I know how passionate you are about your pottery. You should get some exposure."

"Dan getting the kiln in White River Junction is huge. That'll help a lot." Iris added. Faith nodded, smiling.

"But I actually came in to ask you about something else."

"Oh, oh," Faith said, "You're not leaving me, are you?"

"No, no, nothing like that. Man trouble." Iris signed. "Or lack of man trouble."

"Grab some coffee and sit." Faith gestured toward a sofa in the great room. They filled their cups and sat down. The hot coffee mugs felt good in their hands on this chilly afternoon. Sun streamed through the windows and the fall colors were ablaze in the trees. The leaves would be gone before too long, but days like this made Faith glad to be alive.

"First off, what man?" Faith's eyebrows rose up. Iris laughed.

"I know, it's silly, 'cause there really isn't one yet."

"Unless you mean Tom, who's mad about you." Faith became serious.

"Well, you know, it kind of is. I've been thinking about him a lot. I just don't know..." Iris bit her lip.

"What don't you know?"

"How do I communicate with someone who won't make eye contact? How would I ever know what he was feeling or thinking if he were expressionless? And he gets so tongue tied whenever we talk about anything other than flowers..."

"You like him, though?"

"Yes! He's a good guy. He's kind, and a hard worker, and I think he's really sexy in a Vermont mountain man kind of way..."

"And he's obviously crazy about you..."

"Oh, Faith, what should I do? Make the first move? Cause I don't think he'll ever."

Faith nodded. "I think Tom's problem is eye contact. And nerves. What if you began a relationship in a non-traditional way?"

"Like what?"

"How about e-mail? I have friends that swear by online dating. You get to know someone before you even meet them for the first time. Maybe Tom would open up to you online vs. in person."

"How do you start a conversation with someone you're not sure you have anything in common with? And how do you take a conversation anywhere with someone who doesn't get innuendo?" Iris asked.

"You do have stuff in common. The inn. O'Dell. The Christmas Festival. There's stuff you could talk about. Can you do anything with plants or flowers in your pottery? That'd be a start."

"That's an idea. I've thought about making some pieces that look like fossils using plants."

"E-mail him! Do you need his address?" Faith wrote it down on the pad she always had near her.

"I wasn't sure he had one..."

"We do all of our business correspondence via e-mail. Bills, invoices... he's actually quite the computer whiz." Faith smiled. "And as far as the innuendo goes, maybe he won't catch on totally, but he's still a guy."

They giggled as they sipped their coffee.

Later that night Iris composed an e-mail to Tom.

TO: tom.grant@rootsandsky.com
SUBJECT: A Plant Question
FROM: iris@irisparsonspottery.com

Hi Tom,

I was hoping you could help me with a project I'm working on. I'd like to make some of my pots look like they were fossils by imprinting them with either plants, leaves, or flowers. I wanted your opinion on what the best plants to use would be, perhaps ones that weren't too delicate and could stand up to being pressed into clay.

Let me know if you have any ideas.

Thank you!

Iris

77

She hit send and hoped for the best.

THIRTEEN

Kim Edgeworth sat at her kitchen table with the vial of pills in front of her. She knew she needed to take the clozapine as her psychiatrist prescribed it, but she hated the side effects. Mostly it was a headache and sleepiness, but lately there had been some confusion as well. And sometimes when she was confused she couldn't remember if she'd taken one of the doses. Was her relationship with Will real or her imagination? It couldn't be a delusion because somebody was sleeping with her... She could see them together in bed, and all the things they'd done to pleasure each other as real as... as this vial of pills. She picked up her phone and texted. "U were wild in bed," it said, "xxx, Kim."

She'd rescheduled her appointment with her shrink this month, again. There was too much going on at work. Ciaran Lynch was coming and she wanted to make sure all her research was correct and in a fabulous presentation. She needed to get to work. Should she risk another dose? What if she'd already taken it? Better skip it. She checked that the iron was unplugged, twice, washed her hands again for the third time, and left for the office.

Will's phone beeped and he reached for it, unclasping it from his belt. He shook his head.

"What is it?" Faith asked, handing him a cup of coffee. Will and Faith were going over the punch list of the items that needed to be finished up in the Ski Lodge now that the inn rooms were complete.

"Nothing."

Faith felt strange; she had a bad feeling in her gut. It showed on her face.

"Faith, really, it's nothing."

"Fine," she said, still looking troubled. She attempted a smile. "We really should talk. You know, I know that you've been waiting for me and I've been... unavailable. I guess I'd understand if you didn't want to wait anymore..." Faith found herself tearing up, and looked at the ceiling to make the tears retreat.

"What's this really about, Faith?"

"I just feel like I'm being unfair to you. It's obvious Kim is out there and wants you back..." Jack had told Patty he'd found Kim at Will's apartment, and of course Patty had told Faith.

Will sighed and hung his head. Faith wasn't sure if it was resignation, relief... or guilt.

"Obviously you have priorities that differ from mine," he smiled sadly. "You're off the hook, Faith."

"What do you mean?" she asked, tentatively.

"We'll just keep it professional from now on. I won't bother you anymore." Will stormed off to the barn. Faith could feel her heart breaking.

FOURTEEN

Tom was behind in sending an invoice to Faith for the last month, so he sat at his computer to create one. The pop server searched for his latest e-mail and he saw his messages flash quickly in the upper corner of his screen. He saw a message from iris@irisparsonspottery.com and sat straighter in his chair. He clicked on his e-mail icon and brought it up immediately.

He read it. She needed his help. Of course he would help her. He answered immediately.

> TO: iris@irisparsonspottery.com
> SUBJECT: Re: A Plant Question
> FROM: tom.grant@rootsandsky.com

> Hello Iris,
> I will help you with your project. I think ivy, pine, holly and trillium leaves would stand up to the clay. Most flowers would be too fragile. Calla lilies might work but wouldn't look good. I can get some of each of these for you if you want.
> Tom

He liked that she was asking him for help. He hit send and went back to the invoice.

Iris saw Tom's e-mail that night when she got home. Well, it was a start. She wrote back to him.

> TO: tom.grant@rootsandsky.com
> SUBJECT: Re: A Plant Question
> FROM: iris@irisparsonspottery.com

> Tom,
> Thank you for the ideas! Since these pots will be for the Christmas Festival I think holly and pine would be perfect. If it's not too much trouble I'd be grateful if you could get me some cuttings. I'll need them fairly soon as I'll be using the kiln this weekend. When do you think I can get them from you?

Are you getting excited about the Christmas Festival? I know you're going to have a booth there this year. It must be a lot more work for you.

Iris

The next morning Tom wrote back.

TO: iris@irisparsonspottery.com
SUBJECT: Re: A Plant Question
FROM: tom.grant@rootsandsky.com

Hello Iris,
I can bring them by the inn at noon today, or to the studio at 4 or to your house at 5. Please tell me the best time.

I think the booth at the festival is a good opportunity. We'll get more business than we would just at the tree farm. So while it is more work I think it will be worth it.
Tom

Iris checked e-mail when she got up. So Tom-like to be so specific, so cut and dried. Where to meet, then? Maybe the studio would be less threatening.

TO: tom.grant@rootsandsky.com
SUBJECT: Re: A Plant Question
FROM: iris@irisparsonspottery.com

Tom,
Please bring them to the studio at 4. The address is 27 High St. and my studio is in the basement on the right, #3.

The Jay Feather Inn's booth and my booth will be between you and Santa's house at the festival. We'll be neighbors!
Thanks!
Iris

FIFTEEN

The Jay Feather was totally booked for the Christmas Festival, including the not quite yet finished ski lodge above the barn. Faith could have filled two inns between the vendors attending the festival, Thanksgiving, and people visiting O'Dell for the festival. Will was working night and day to get the work done so Faith and her crew could clean, decorate and ready the place for guests. The lodge was great for ski teams or families as it had rooms with lots of beds, even bunk beds. There was a shared shower room with multiple stalls like a gym or dorm. And the rough pine walls and beamed ceilings made it feel like what it was: a bunkhouse.

Faith was going to keep the décor simple and inexpensive. She'd heard too many stories from Jack about the roughhousing that went on when ski teams traveled together, so she was having Will build the bed frames into the structure as platforms. They wouldn't move no matter what these kids did to them. One of Will's friends made Faith some Adirondack chairs using broken skis and hockey sticks that were colorful, whimsical and perfect in the rooms and common area. She'd found some corrugated ski resort sign reproductions that could be bolted to the walls. And while she was a fan of natural fiber and down pillows and comforters she was not going to risk using really expensive stuff up there. Foam pillows wouldn't spew feathers in a pillow fight, and fleece blankets were warm and easily laundered. Let them have fun, and no harm no foul if something was damaged, it wasn't expensive to begin with.

Faith was moving forward with all of her plans for the inn and the festival, but she was still heartbroken about Will and continued to have this feeling in the pit of her stomach about the mortgage and Kim Edgeworth's threat. Her lawyers were taking their time getting back to her. Her grandfather's advisers found her the best mortgage rate; she hoped they'd found a reputable bank. There was nothing she'd accomplish by worrying about it and she did have the offer of loans from Jack and her mom, but she did wonder if she were just rearranging deck chairs on the Titanic.

Just as she pushed the feelings away once more her cell phone rang. She saw it was her lawyer's office calling.

"This is Faith."

"Hi Faith, Its Brian Waverly."

"Brian, please tell me the news is good."

Silence. Faith's heart sank.

"Well, we have good and bad news. One of the mortgage company's largest investors is CLI, so they do have some leverage. And the fine print does say that under certain circumstances Worldwide Mortgage can pull your loan."

"What's the good news?"

"They haven't. There has been no movement in that direction at all, and I have good contacts inside there. That doesn't mean they won't, but at this point you're OK."

"That may not last, though."

"You're right, but it gives Jack Kimball and your mom the chance to liquidate some assets and us a chance to get the paperwork ready so if they do pull the note you won't risk default."

"And I guess it gives me an opportunity to arrange alternate financing..."

"Well, Faith, it would depend on timing. If the bank pulls the loan while your application with a new mortgage company is in process it won't look good. If they think there was a default or an issue with cash flow you might not get a new loan, or the terms might be so bad you wouldn't want it."

Faith felt the tears come to her eyes. She steadied her voice and said, "My actual business is better than my initial projections. This is just crazy. If I can't refinance then I'd never be able to pay Jack and my mom back other than treating them as though they held a traditional mortgage. Neither of them is going to be willing to wait 30 years for their money."

"I guess it depends on the interest rate and how much they need the principal."

"This was supposed to be short term," she whispered.

"Faith, I know you have your heart set on The Jay Feather, but maybe you should hear CLI out. If they make an offer it might be worth your while. They'll probably try that before resorting to having the bank cancel your mortgage."

"I guess I don't have a choice." Faith felt defeated.

Faith met with Jack and Patty to tell them the news.

"CLI is a major stockholder with the mortgage company. They could possibly have my loan pulled."

84

"*Who* is the parent company of The Overlook?" Patty asked, looking stricken.

"CLI. I don't know anything about them; they're not a big player in the US. Or at least not yet, based on what Kim said." Faith furrowed her brow. "Why?"

"Nothing," Patty said. "So what? I promised you a loan and I'll give you a loan."

"I don't touch my money anyway," Jack chimed in. "The interest would make this a safe investment for me. I'm still in."

"You're both wonderful to offer, but I don't think I could live with myself." Faith's eyes filled with tears.

"Sweetie, just think about it. Sleep on it. Don't say yes or no right now. It's been a long day, you might feel differently tomorrow."

It was late afternoon and guests were starting to wander in for cocktails. Buck was at the bar nursing a beer. It was Iris's day off, so Faith had bartender duty. She tried to shake off her feeling of defeat and put on her best smile. Jack and Patty followed her into the bar.

Jack sat at the bar and had Faith pour him his usual, and Patty helped out as waitress until Kendra came in at 4:30. Buck's eyes followed Faith as she worked. She looked at him to see if he wanted a refill. He nodded. She put the fresh glass down in front of him.

"What's wrong, my pretty?" Buck had grabbed her hand. Jack was watching closely.

"Not a blessed thing, Buck. How's it going with you?" she asked as she extracted herself from his grip.

"I don't believe you," he said under his breath. "Anything I can do?"

Faith thought there was any number of things he could do. Leave her the hell alone and stop creeping her out for starters. She smiled her best hospitality industry smile.

"Sweet of you to ask, Buck, but no. Thank you anyway."

"Anytime... Anything... Just say the word." His look made her shiver. She walked away. Faith looked up at two gentlemen entering the bar and smiled.

"Gus! You made it down to visit me!" Faith came around the bar and gave him a kiss on the cheek. It was the best thing that had happened all day.

"I told you I would, so here I am. This here is my nephew Sandy Gregson. He's a doctor down in Montpelier and he's here to check up on me."

"Just a visit, Uncle Gus. I haven't even taken your blood pressure."

"He's the one suggested we come for a drink. Used to stay here as a kid when he was on the Waterbury ski team," Gus added.

"Wow, welcome back," Faith said as she shook his hand.

"I remember you," Jack said, squinting at him. "You were their star slalom racer in 1998."

"Good memory. You were O'Dell's coach, weren't you?" Sandy asked.

"Still am! I didn't realize you were Gus's nephew."

"Yup," Gus said. "My sister's boy. So, young lady, I hear you have some nice whiskey."

Faith showed Gus and Sandy to a table with comfortable chairs, and they asked Jack to join them.

"Sandy, are you a whiskey drinker as well?" Faith asked from back behind the bar.

"That'd be great!"

"Rocks or neat?" She held up a bottle of Whistle Pig, a locally distilled rye whiskey. Sandy smiled.

"Awesome! Rocks for me, neat for Uncle Gus."

She brought their glasses over and watched Gus take a long sniff and an appreciative mouthful.

"Well, they were right. You do have some nice whiskey down here." They all laughed.

Sandy watched his uncle enjoying his drink and conversing with his new friend Faith. She was a looker. He wondered if she was spoken for. Just then he saw Will Grant coming in through the kitchen.

"Oh my God, I can't believe it!" Will laughed as he came and shook Sandy's hand. "Sandy Gregson as I live and breathe!"

Sandy laughed and stood up. "Jesus, Will, I thought you'd be long gone by now with that fancy MBA of yours."

"Nope, decided to stay put and do what I love."

"Which is?"

"I'm a contractor. And I own Roots and Sky Nursery and Tree Farm. And you? Are you Doctor Gregson now?"

"You got it. Gifford Medical Center. I'm here visiting my Uncle Gus."

"Hi, Gus." Will put out his hand. "I see your beard's doing nicely. Now we just need to fatten you up."

"Why?" Faith asked handing Will a Shed IPA. It was not lost on Sandy that she knew what Will drank.

"He's the O'Dell Christmas Festival's Santa. Has been for 15 years now," Jack said.

"That's great," Faith said, "you're perfect for it!"

"But we need a Mrs. Santa this year, and we haven't found her yet," Jack said. "Gladys Gibbons moved to Florida this past winter. Got any suggestions?"

Faith smiled but shook her head.

Will joined the table and caught up with his old rival. And the way Sandy's eye kept moving back to Faith he wondered if he was going to be a rival in more than skiing. For even though he had told Faith their relationship was purely professional he'd done it for her sake, not his. There were things he regretted recently, but telling Faith it was over he regretted most, ever since the words left his lips.

SIXTEEN

Tom showed up at Iris's studio exactly at 4PM carrying two industrial trash bags filled with cuttings. Iris couldn't help but laugh when she opened the door and saw him standing there. Tom looked very concerned.

"Did I do the wrong thing?" he asked.

"No, oh no, no, no," she laughed. "I just didn't expect that you'd bring so much! It's great!" Tom looked relieved. "Come in! Let me show you what I was planning."

He followed her in and set down the bags. Every surface of her studio was covered with soup bowls sitting upside down waiting for an imprint and some glaze.

"I was hoping I could do the imprints like this..." She reached into one of the bags and pulled out a holly leaf with berries. She positioned it in a way she thought was pleasing and pressed the plant into the side. The clay was wet enough to accept an imprint but dry enough not to stick. The effect was quite pretty. Tom looked in wonder at the bowl.

"You can't reuse them," he said. "I can see little bits of sand on the leaf. You'll need to use a new one each time."

"Then it's a good thing you brought so many!" She smiled at him. He looked nervous, but he smiled back, just a little.

"I can help you. If you want."

"I could use it! Can you stay now?"

"Yes." He was studying the pots.

"Would you like a cup of tea?" she asked.

"Yes. Thank you."

While she made tea he pulled a pine bough from the bag, and looked at one of the bowls intently.

"Wow! It smells like Christmas in here!" she said.

"And you like Christmas?" he asked. She nodded enthusiastically. He looked at the bowl and pine needles again.

"You can't make a mistake, Tom. If it gets messed up and I can't correct it then I'll use the pot it in a mosaic. So don't be afraid, just go for it."

He looked calmer. He pressed the two pronged pine bough into the clay, and carefully removed it. He smiled.

Iris handed him a cup. "That's perfect!"

88

"What temperature is the kiln?" he asked.

"About 1900 degrees."

"I wonder what it would look like if you left them in the pot and let the fire burn the plants away?"

"Well, interesting idea," she said, "but it could get messy with the sap and water in the plants. So I probably won't try that. Thanks for the idea, though."

They worked together for the next few hours. Iris put some jazz on the stereo. They worked from surface to surface in opposite directions and when they came together they were back to back. Other than a question or two they hadn't spoken, just traded glances and shy smiles. Tom finished his last pot before Iris, and turned around, looking over her shoulder.

"Nice," he said. She turned her head and looked up at him. And held his gaze. He didn't look away this time. He reached down and wiped a pine needle off of her cheek. She smiled. And sure enough, he really was still just a guy; he leaned down and kissed her.

SEVENTEEN

Patty sat rocking in one of the white rockers on The Jay Feather's porch. It was late and very dark, the mountain air was chilly. She'd taken one of the wool throws out with her and had it wrapped around her like a shawl. She didn't know what to do. She hadn't realized that the parent company of The Overlook Hotel was CLI, and she knew what CLI stood for, but she was betting Faith didn't. Ciaran Lynch was Faith's father. How could she tell her daughter that her own father was trying to take her new business from her? Maybe she didn't have to. Maybe if she and Jack just gave Faith the loans Faith would never find out.

Patty knew Faith had never been curious about her father outwardly, but in the age of the Internet there was no guarantee that Faith hadn't Googled him. Patty had. That's how she knew he was the CEO of a very healthy worldwide property company specializing in hotels.

Patty had had no intention of ever contacting him. She wasn't a gold digger; she'd never asked him for a cent and never would, not that it wouldn't have been handy in the early years. Thank the heavens for her parents. But it did sometimes bother her that he didn't even know he had a daughter. This beautiful, smart, funny, amazing young woman who looked like him and shared his mannerisms. And did Faith have siblings out there? It wasn't fair to Faith not to know for sure. But Patty still didn't know how she was going to handle this, she just hoped Faith would take the money she and Jack offered so she wouldn't have to worry about it. Should she contact Ciaran and ask him to back off?

The door creaked open and Faith came outside. The inn guests were all in their rooms and the bar was closed for the night. She joined her mom on the porch.

"Nice night," Faith whispered.

"It is pretty out here. Look at the stars!"

They sat and rocked, gazing at the heavens.

"So, you want to tell me what's going on?" Faith eventually asked.

"You go first." Patty knew her daughter was more troubled than usual.

"No. You've been somewhere else all evening. Preoccupied. Jack noticed, too. I could tell by the way he was watching you. Is it about the money?"

"No, Sweetie, it's not. That money, which I hope you'll take, is all yours."

"You know what, mom? I'm going to try to fight them. I bet they wouldn't like it if someone shone a big, bright light on their dealings. Exposed them for what they are."

Patty hung her head. "Honey, they're a privately held organization. There are no public stockholders to get incensed over their behavior. It might be a blip on the radar for them if they get badmouthed in a news cast, and then business as usual."

"This doesn't sound like you, mom. What's really going on?"

"Just tired, I guess. Work's been crazy, I should be inside reviewing a report right now but it's just so nice out here."

"You're sure everything's OK?"

"It's fine. Now what's going on with you?"

Faith started to cry. She told her mom about her conversation with Will, and how things were left.

"Give it time, Sweetie. I think you both have too much going on right now. I think he's crazy about you. He didn't stop looking at you all night."

Faith sighed. Patty got up and reached out for her beautiful girl. They walked into the inn, their arms around each other.

Kim had waited up and left the porch light on. It was late, but she knew he'd come back. She was in bed, lying in the dark, naked. She heard the door and his footsteps in the hall. He hadn't turned the lights on. Her eyes had adjusted to the dark and she could make out his body in the doorway. She watched him undress. He said nothing, but he watched her watching him. He slid into the bed next to her. Without a word he grabbed her face in his hands and kissed her deep and hard. He sucked on her tongue and moved against her body. He fondled her breast and moved his mouth down to her nipple. She gasped when he bit her, and he pushed his head tighter to her, doing it again. He pulled her legs apart quickly and roughly. She knew what would come next. He slid into her hard. She gasped again. He pulled her arms over

91

her head and held her captive as he fucked her. She wrapped her legs around him, working herself on him, losing herself in the pleasure and the fear. He knew how she liked it. She came quickly and violently, and her climax brought him near the edge. He watched her face contort, and he let himself go, pounding her faster and faster as he came. He lay on top of her as their breathing slowed. He rolled off of her and slid out of bed. She watched him dress without a word. He put an envelope on the table and he slipped out of the house as silently as he entered.

Will checked on Tom when he got home, and his room was empty. He knew he was meeting Iris that afternoon, and he hoped his brother was holding his own on what could be his first date. He was happy it was Iris; she was always good to Tom and she was a good person. She wouldn't jerk him around. Was that what he was doing with Faith? Was he jerking her around? He wasn't happy with the current situation, any of it, but he wasn't sure what to do.

Iris had taken Tom back to her apartment. She cooked him dinner while he sat at her kitchen table and had a beer. She kept up most of the conversation but he seemed happy to let her do it. Even smiling at her when she looked at him. She sensed that the only way to communicate with Tom would be directly and literally, without innuendo or sarcasm. It was a stretch for her, as she had a knack for cracking wise, but she felt in her heart that Tom was worth the effort.

After dinner they sat on her sofa and talked for a while.

"Tom, I really like you," she started. He smiled. "Are you having a good time, hanging out with me like this?"

He beamed.

"Yes. I like you, Iris. A lot. Can we do this? Um, spend time together?" He spoke slowly, measured.

"I'd like that." She stroked his cheek and he reached up and put his hand over hers.

"Can I kiss you again?" he asked, looking like he'd been looking forward to it all evening. She nodded. He leaned down and kissed her, once softly, and then again. She held his face and kissed him, letting him know it was all right. She thought to herself that he probably hadn't had much experience, and it made her excited to perhaps be his teacher. It was as though he'd read her thoughts.

"Iris," he started, "I, um, haven't really, um, done this..."

"It's OK, Tom. Do you want to...?" she started to ask, but he cut her off.

"Yes."

She giggled.

"Good," she said. "Me, too."

And with that she began Tom's education. They kissed and petted. She told him where it felt good to be kissed and touched. She explored his body as they shed their clothes, slowly exposing themselves to each other. She wondered if they would actually make love tonight. It didn't matter, but she wanted him to be comfortable and set the pace. Would this all be overwhelming to him? Or as Faith had said, is he still just a guy and be up for sex no matter the circumstance?

He was awed by her breasts and couldn't get enough of touching and fondling them. She thought he might climax from that alone, and she knew whatever happened he'd climax quickly this first time. She rose and reached her hands out to him. His look of arousal made her weak. She brought him to her bed, and they lay next to each other, kissing and touching.

"Can I?" he asked. She nodded. He knew what to do, even though he probably hadn't done it before. She opened herself to him and guided him. The halting gasp of surprise in his voice made her melt. She instructed him with her hips, he found their rhythm. To her surprise he wasn't shy here; he watched her face as he moved in her, looking awed by what they were doing and how it felt, and how she reacted to his movements. The teacher became the student, experiencing lovemaking so differently than ever before. The feeling and the intensity overwhelmed her and she began to climax. He was smiling at her and kissed her as he continued to thrust. She could feel his intensity build, and finally his orgasm overtook him. He finally slowed and stopped, kissing her over and over again. They rolled to their sides, facing each other.

He smiled.

"Can we do that again?"

EIGHTEEN

Faith awoke at her usual time and headed out for her run. As she made her way up the hill she could see wood smoke from Gus's house and a car in the yard. It must be Sandy's, she thought. She heard her blue jay before she could see him, like clockwork he'd appear in Gus's yard and wait for her. She smiled. As she stopped to say good morning to her jay and say a prayer for her grandfather she heard Gus's door slam. Sandy, dressed in running clothes, came out to meet her. His black running tights hugged his thighs and the blue fleece pullover made his eyes shine. He was a very attractive package.

"I hear there's a routine..." His eyes were smiling. "Do you mind some company?"

"Not at all! Just give me a sec." She said a quick prayer and blew a kiss to her blue jay.

"Gus told me that's your grandfather?" He was really smiling now.

"Well... yeah. It makes me happy to think he's looking after me. And even if it's just a reminder to say a prayer for him I think it's all good," she huffed as their pace picked up.

"Hey," he panted as they crested the hill, "I say hi to Aunt Muriel every time I come."

"The cardinal?"

"Yup."

They ran in silence for a bit.

"So. I have to ask," he puffed.

"Oh, oh." She smiled.

"Are you and Will...?" He turned to watch her.

She shook her head.

"Could have fooled me," he laughed.

"Why?"

"He watched you all night. But if you're telling me you aren't then is there a chance...?"

Faith interrupted him. "Not really. I have to focus on my business. But I'm flattered!"

"Too bad. Gus would have been thrilled, too." He smiled at her. "Thanks for being a friend to him, by the way."

"Your uncle is great. He is so like my grandfather," she huffed, "I'm glad he's playing Santa. Our booth will be right next to Santa's house. Are you coming to the Christmas Festival?"

"Wouldn't miss it."

As they ran the loop back toward the main road there were enough leaves off of the trees that Faith could see the back of the inn in the distance. She stopped short.

"You OK?" Sandy asked with his hands on his knees, catching his breath.

"Can you see that?" She pointed to a car on the logging road behind the inn. Sandy moved to the left a bit for a better view.

"What is that? A limo?"

"Yup." She could see there was a man standing next to it with binoculars, studying the inn.

"Do you know what that's about?" he asked.

"I have a hunch." Faith started to run again and Sandy was right behind her. They'd need to cover a fair amount of ground to get to the logging road from where they'd stopped. Before they could get there the limo started and pulled away. Faith wondered if it would stop at the inn, but instead it took a right and headed north, in the direction of The Overlook.

Faith and Sandy got to the bottom of the road and watched the limo drive away.

"Are you alright?" Sandy asked as they approached the inn. "I can come in and hang for awhile if you need someone to talk to," he offered.

"Thanks. Do you want coffee? I put some on before I left."

"Sure!"

They entered the quiet foyer and saw Rita setting tables in the dining room. They could smell the coffee and followed their noses to the breakfront where the coffee urns sat. They each grabbed a cup and sat in front of the fire in the great room. Sandy peeled off his fleece pullover to expose a tight fitting moisture-wicking tee shirt and an impressive set of abs. Sandy asked about the limo. Faith told him the story of CLI, the bank and Kim Edgeworth.

"Will's fiancée?"

"Ex, but yes."

"She had a psychotic break."

"You knew about that?"

95

"I did. She was hospitalized. And stabilized, I thought."

"She seems stable now. But she's been acting a little weird toward Will. She told Will she's on medication."

"She'd have to be. Nasty stuff, some of the meds; terrible side effects. Weight gain, confusion, headaches, lethargy."

"Really?" Faith asked.

"Yes. I don't envy my patients that take anti-psychotics. They have to be closely monitored. Things can go bad really fast if the dose isn't correct."

"What kind of doctor are you?"

"Psychiatrist."

"Then I guess you would know about this."

"Actually, Kim's case is what got me interested in the specialty. She heard voices. It was terrible to see what it did to her. Do you think she was in the limo?"

"I think it must have been someone from CLI in the limo," she said. "Who else would be looking the place over?"

"Private investigator?" he joked. "Someone staying here with the wrong spouse?"

Faith laughed. "You see all kinds of things in this business. And it's amazing what people leave behind."

"Like?"

"Vibrators."

Sandy choked on his coffee.

"Sex toys. Stuff like that. You can't really send them back. They'd be horrified to know you'd found them. And if they were with someone they weren't supposed to be with and the unsuspecting wife or husband gets the package then... Well, you get the picture."

Sandy nodded.

"You want breakfast? I smell bacon. I think Delroy's making blueberry pancakes this morning."

"Thanks, but I'm going to head back and have breakfast with Gus. Thanks for the coffee. And if you change your mind..." he smiled.

Faith blushed. "You're a shameless flirt." She grinned as he left.

Iris passed Sandy Gregson in the parking lot as he jogged toward his uncle's house. She was watching his butt

96

as she opened the door. Rita was standing there doing the same.

"He's too young for me but, boy, wouldn't he be fun to play with."

"Rita!" Iris laughed as she swatted her with the back of her hand. "Who is he?"

"Sandy Gregson. Doctor Gregson. Gus Norman's nephew."

"What was he doing here? Is he staying with us?"

"No, he and Faith came in from a run together. Better ask her." Rita smiled and raised her eyebrows as Iris walked toward the kitchen.

Faith had a cup of coffee in one hand and a slice of bacon in the other. She was sitting on a stool in the kitchen by the woodstove as Delroy whipped up the pancake batter.

"You're in early," Faith said to Iris. "How did it go yesterday?" Faith tilted her head at her friend.

"Um, gooood." She smiled.

"WHOO HOO!" Faith jumped up and did the happy dance. It was the first happy thought Faith had experienced this week. Delroy chuckled. "So? Spill!" Faith demanded.

"You were right. He's definitely a guy." Iris blushed.

"Me a go outside if you be talking about your ag-o-ny," Delroy whispered.

"What?" Iris asked. Faith burst out laughing.

"Ag-o-ny is Jamaican slang for an orgasm," Faith managed to laugh out.

"*How* do you know that?" Iris asked, incredulous.

"A year at the Tryall Club in Montego Bay. I learned a LOT."

"Well, I will NOT be talking about my 'ag-o-ny', Delroy, so settle down."

"Irie, mon."

"What I do want to talk about is how did you end up running with Gus's nephew this morning?" Iris asked Faith.

"I guess Gus told him about my morning run. He came out of the cabin when he saw me. Good thing, too. I have a witness who can also say he saw a guy outside a black limo on the access road behind the inn this morning. With binoculars."

"What?" Delroy and Iris said in unison.

"Not sure what's going on but I have a feeling we'll know soon..."

97

Kim knew today was a big day for her. Ciaran Lynch and Randy Preston were due in to review Kim's presentation and make some decisions on which properties to go after. She had only met Mr. Lynch a couple of times and wanted to make a good impression. She'd been rehearsing her speech for days, and stayed up most nights to perfect it. She was going to ace this presentation. Her bosses would be awed by her. She'd get a promotion. She felt so good about everything she'd decided it was OK to cut back on her medication. It made her so confused and lethargic. And she felt so much better without so much of it in her system. It certainly kept her even, no highs and lows, but she loved the highs so much why should she live without them? She felt great. She was thinking about the sex. She liked it but she knew she shouldn't. It confused her. No, wait. Hadn't she practiced her speech all night? No, he was there. She knew it.

NINETEEN

Ciaran Lynch and his family flew into Boston but instead of parting company with them so that Marthe and Brendan could look at schools as originally planned Ciaran decided to stay and spend a few days doing it with them. They toured Boston College, BU, MIT, Tufts and Harvard. They ate seafood, visited museums, enjoyed the city, and laughed at the accents and especially at the Massachusetts Department of Transportation's signs on the highways to encourage drivers changing lanes to operate their directional signals.

The signs read, *"Changing lanes? Use yah blinkah!"*

When it was time to head to Vermont they went all together, in a rented SUV.

The foliage was beautiful but past it's peak in the Boston area. They knew there would be less color and fewer leaves the further north they drove, but New England was picturesque nonetheless. It was Ciaran's plan to take the scenic route and visit each of the properties Randy Preston and Kim Edgeworth had forwarded to him, that way he'd have a visual that was more than just a photo of the place when he listened to their presentation. He wanted to know what the towns were like, if there was competition in the area and what it looked like. He wanted to know if there were attractions to keep people occupied or if CLI would have to expend additional capital to provide entertainment for the guests. Could a nearby school require guest rooms for parents? And how often could that occupancy be counted on? And he knew all of that would be covered in the dossier on each property. But beyond that Ciaran trusted his gut and could tell if a property had potential almost immediately upon seeing it. He could feel its energy. Which is why he vetted every property CLI bought personally, and why he traveled so much. Had they bought properties that had failed? Very few, and it usually happened when the deal looked so good Ciaran had blessed it without making his normal visit. This time they were going in a completely different direction and he wanted to be sure he was comfortable with the transaction. So he'd planned a six-day trip where they would stay in each property for the night,

99

checking in under Marthe's name so as not to alert any savvy business owner to his identity. Few even knew CLI would be making them an offer. Yet.

Their week was more enjoyable than Ciaran could have hoped. They visited quaint Vermont towns with apple orchards and harvest fairs. Small shops with unique items unavailable in big commercial shopping centers, art galleries, organic restaurants with menus that changed daily, antique shops in old barns, and college towns that Brendan had never even heard of. The inns were comfortable but certainly needed upgrades. The food in most was above average, but many only served one offering. Some were BYOB; he'd need to pay close attention as to whether his people had investigated liquor licenses. He would be interested in hearing how his staff was going to pitch this and he wanted to see the numbers. He wasn't sure the plan made sense, but he'd had a good week with his family so that was something.

They had one more stop, in O'Dell at The Jay Feather Inn. The place they'd stayed the night before was very close to O'Dell so Randy Preston sent a limo for Ciaran as their meeting was early in the morning. Ciaran knew he'd not have all the data he needed, as he hadn't stayed at the last inn yet, but his decision wouldn't be made instantaneously. He'd be able to experience O'Dell before deciding on the plan. Marthe and Brendan would take the rented SUV and spend some time hiking and then poking around in the center of O'Dell before checking in later in the day. Ciaran would meet them at the inn and they'd have dinner together.

Ciaran asked the limo driver if O'Dell was on the way to The Overlook. Since it was not far out of the way he asked the driver to take him past The Jay Feather. The limo driver offered to drive up the logging road in the back for a better view. Ciaran liked the look of the place. It had obviously been well kept and had some recent renovation. As they drove around the property Ciaran could see lights on in many windows; business was obviously good. He stepped out and looked through his binoculars. A fire in the fireplace, activity in the kitchen, and wood smoke from the chimneys all showed the promise of a busy establishment. And there was something about the place. His gut was working overtime as he tilted his head and wiggled his fingers. A blue jay alit on a nearby branch and squawked at him.

TWENTY

Will came into the kitchen with Hank close behind. Peaches and Herb had just finished their breakfast in the mudroom and sat giving each other a bath, so Hank joined the party, knocking Peaches over with his first lick. She didn't seem to mind.

"Morning Delroy, is Faith around?" Will asked.

"Soon come, mon. Coffee?"

Will nodded and helped himself to a thermos pot Delroy kept in the kitchen where he sometimes brewed his private stash of Jamaican Blue Mountain.

"Nothin' but coffee in here, right, man?" Will grinned. Delroy laughed.

"Is all irie, mon. You be safe."

Faith walked in, freshly showered with her hair still damp. Will just stared at her, she was so lovely.

"Good morning." She was tentative. "Do you have time to review the punch list with me or are you headed right to the barn?"

"Beautiful, I always have time for you." He said the words before he could stop himself. Faith looked like she might cry.

"Is gettin' thick in here, mon." Delroy quipped from the stove, not knowing they had parted. Will walked with Faith to the library. On the way they saw guests enjoying breakfast and Iris and Rita pouring coffee in the dining room.

"Where's Patty?" Will asked.

"Where do you think?" Faith said quietly. It killed him that she felt so distant.

"Wait. She was here last night when Jack and I left..."

"I woke up to find a note that said she'd gone to Jack's and she'd see me later."

"Wow. Booty call. At their age." Will couldn't help but grin. Faith swatted him.

"My mother is not old."

"No, she's not. And she's hot. Bodes well for me."

"How so?" She looked sideways at him.

"I know you'll be hot when you're her age." Will grabbed Faith and kissed her. She pulled back.

"What are you doing? My head's spinning. I thought..."

"I know. Sorry. I just can't help myself when I'm around you." Will took her into his arms and kissed her again.

Faith wanted him, too. But could she trust him? Was he involved with Kim? Something was going on, but she didn't know what. Did she really want to know? She looked deep into his eyes and kissed him. She was trying to figure out if this was lust or love, and if she'd be sorry about this in the end. She started to pull away.

"Mmm. Slow down, Will. This feels really good but I don't know what's going on with you. Us. I want this to be right if it's going to happen. I don't want secrets and suspicion, and I don't want to be making these decisions in the middle of a business crisis."

"You're right," he said. He knew she was right, and he felt he couldn't give her what she needed right now. But he wanted her nonetheless. He backed away. It killed him to let her go. "So. Punch list?"

"Um, yeah. By the way, something strange happened this morning. Someone in a limo was on the logging road behind the inn when I went for my run. They were looking at the place with binoculars."

"What? Call your lawyer and find out if he's heard anything new. And take the loans from Patty and Jack."

Faith told him what her lawyer had said about the possibility of not getting a new loan.

"Maybe not right now, Faith, but probably not forever. Take the loans from Jack and your mom. You have collateral. Maybe interest rates won't be as low in a few years but you'll have built up your business, won't need as much money and be in a better position to bargain."

"I keep forgetting you have an MBA." She smiled, but she was just going through the motions. This was all so overwhelming. She wanted him so badly but wished she'd just kept him at a distance from the start.

Patty was sitting on Jack's kitchen counter as he poured and handed her a cup of coffee. Before she got to take a sip he was pulling her towards him and kissing her. She wrapped her legs around him and kissed him back, her hands caressing his naked chest. She wanted to think of anything but the inn or CLI and this was a fine way to keep her mind off of her problems. Jack was happy to oblige. Patty was wearing nothing but Jack's pajama top so by undoing a few buttons he had total access. He loved her full breasts and how with little effort he could make her nipples hard. He loved that she was aroused so easily. He kissed and bit her neck, as he caressed her soft breasts. By her moans he knew he had permission to go further. He eased himself out of his pajama bottoms and cupped her bottom, tilting her up as he entered her. She shuddered with delight.

"Oh, yes," she whispered. He moved slowly at first, feeling her heat rise. "More," she pled. He moved deeper and faster as she pulled him into her with her legs. It didn't take long for her to start her pant, the sound Jack knew meant she was close, and finally her head fell back as she came. He continued to move with her, knowing he could make her come again, and she obliged with pleasure before he felt his own orgasm rise and sweep over him. They stilled, panting, wrapped around each other against the kitchen counter.

"That was... delicious," she whispered.

"Wasn't it, now?" he replied.

They showered together and tried another go at coffee, sitting at Jack's kitchen table fully clothed.

"I'm glad you called me last night," he said. "I've missed you."

"Thanks for coming to get me. I was afraid you'd be asleep."

"No, actually I was just lying there thinking about you. And since we didn't get a chance to talk last night..."

"No, we sure didn't do much talking," she interrupted. Patty had been very needy; there had been little talk and less sleep.

"So lets talk now. What's going around in that beautiful head of yours?" He grabbed her hand. Patty hung her head. "You know you can talk to me about anything," he added.

"Oh, Jack. Can I?" She looked confused.

"Of course." He'd realized he was madly in love with this woman the last time she left for New York. He hadn't told her because he didn't want to scare her away. Now he looked at her and saw she was obviously conflicted about something. Was it them? He waited in silence for her to decide what to say.

"I," she paused. "I'm telling you something I haven't even told Faith. And somehow I feel like I'm betraying her."

Jack got nervous. "Are you alright? Are you ill... or," he didn't know how to ask.

"No, nothing like that. I'm fine." She smiled sadly at him.

"If you feel like you need to talk to Faith first..."

"That's the problem. I don't know what to do. It would be good to have someone to bounce this off of, but I'd be asking you to keep a pretty volatile secret..."

"I'd do anything for you," he whispered. She took his hand in hers and kissed it.

"Thank you. Well, here goes. You know the company that owns The Overlook? CLI?"

"Certainly."

"CLI stands for Ciaran Lynch International. Ciaran Lynch is Faith's father."

Jack's chin fell.

"Talk about a bombshell... My God, Patty, how long have you known?"

"Since yesterday. Everyone kept talking about the parent company of The Overlook, but no one had said the name."

"What are you going to do?"

"I have no idea." Patty shared her feelings with Jack about her sadness that Ciaran didn't know his daughter. And that she wasn't sure if she should contact him.

"You're going for the let sleeping dogs lie approach?" he asked.

"I just wish she'd take the money from us so she never has to know."

"But she doesn't get a choice that way. Shouldn't she have a say?"

"I don't know!" she wailed. "Should I have told him about her from the time I was pregnant? There are so many things that could have been different..."

"But they're not; spilled milk and all that. Let it go. Now is the only thing you have to work with."

TWENTY ONE

Marthe and Brendon hiked part of the Long Trail after Ciaran left in the morning. The mountain air was chilly but the bright sunshine warmed their backs, and the fresh air and strenuous hike made them ravenous for lunch. They wanted to explore O'Dell and made their first stop at The Buttery Scone for lunch. Kendra was working the lunch shift that day, and waited their table. She and Brendan traded shy smiles.

"What do you recommend?" Marthe asked.

"Well, everything is home made. All of our turkey, ham and roast beef is roasted here; it's not deli meat. So the turkey club and the roast beef and Swiss are really good. Our burgers are really good, too."

"What's your favorite?" Brendan asked.

"It's weird."

"Tell me," he smiled.

"I like our grilled turkey, Swiss and cranberry mayo, but I also put jalapeños and mustard on it." She giggled.

"What's your name?" Brendan asked.

"Kendra."

"I'm Brendan. And I'll have the Kendra special, then." He closed his menu. "And what's a frappe?"

"A milkshake with ice cream in it."

"I'll have a chocolate one, please." He smiled.

"So glad you're so decisive, darling," Marthe said. "Hmm, I'll have the green salad with grilled chicken. And a cup of tea. Earl Grey if you have it." Kendra nodded. She took their menus.

"I'll be right back with your drinks."

Marthe smiled at Brendan as he watched Kendra walk away. He'd had girls he'd gone to school with and who were in his circle of friends, but never a real girlfriend. She hoped he wasn't going to get his heart broken in New England.

Kendra returned shortly with Marthe's tea and Brendan's frappe, which she served in an old-fashioned soda fountain glass with the extra in the stainless malt cup it was made in. And there was a lot of extra.

"Try it. Tell me if it's OK," she said. It was so thick he could barely suck it through the straw. He feigned lightheadedness. Kendra laughed.

"It's brilliant! Really good."

"So Kendra, are you in school?" Marthe asked.

"Yes, I'm a sophomore at Green Mountain High."

"College bound?" she asked.

"I hope so. I'm trying to save as much as I can, and I'm hoping for scholarships. I work here sometimes and most nights at The Jay Feather Inn."

"We're staying there tonight," Brendan said. "Do you wait tables there?"

"Yes! Ask for me!"

"We will!"

Ciaran's day was not going as well as his wife and son's. While the dossiers on each of the properties were complete there was no chance at liquor licenses for a couple of the properties, one of which was owned outright by the innkeeper, who would be looking for much more than the property was worth to sell. Another had a property inspection on file with the bank and needed serious infrastructure repairs. So far only two of the six were worth pursuing, and he hadn't seen the sixth one at all yet, but its numbers did look good. Worldwide Mortgage held the note on this property so CLI got an inside peek at their financials. Their occupancy rates were over their initial projections and they were paying their bills on time. He'd see what it was like when he stayed at The Jay Feather Inn tonight.

Kimberly Edgeworth had done most of the presentation, with Randy Preston jumping in as necessary. Ciaran had met her before, but she seemed on edge. Just nerves? Or something else? He wasn't sure, but he felt bad for the lass. After the meeting he met privately with Randy.

"Ciaran, I know you're not happy with some of the intel we gathered..."

"No, Randy, I'm not. I thought you had six solid properties and now we may not even have three."

"There are others, it's just that we might need to put a bit more money into renovations and their locations might be further apart than the original plan."

106

"How quickly can you put the list and a dossier together? I'm here now, I may as well stay this week to get this resolved."

"I'll have Kim pull them together immediately."

"Do you have anyone to help her? She seems, I don't know. Out of sorts. A bit wild eyed." Ciaran said.

"I'll help her myself. We won't disappoint you, sir."

"Good. Now get me a lift to go join my family."

Marthe and Brendan drove the long drive to The Jay Feather Inn in the mid afternoon. The sun was almost behind the mountain and Marthe thought how much it was like the Alps, where the days in the mountains were very short. Beautiful, but short. As they parked a big Akita trotted over. They saw a worker come out of the barn and head for a pickup truck.

"C'mon Hank," Will called. The dog walked up to Brendan and dropped his front paws to the ground, like he wanted to play. He made the yip and howl noise he saved for his approach to the inn. Will walked over to the SUV.

"I'm sorry, he never does this."

"He's beautiful," Marthe said. Brendan crouched down and rubbed Hank's ears.

"What's his name?" Brendan asked.

"Hank. And he's acting weird. He only makes that noise when he knows he's going to see Faith, the owner here. Though I gotta tell you, you look a lot like her," Will said to Brendan.

"Really?" Marthe asked.

"Yuh, same dark hair and eyes, wow. Yuh. A lot. Hank, c'mon, I need a shower and I've got stuff to do tonight." Hank got up and with a last whine and yip headed to the truck.

"Goofball," Will said to him as he walked by. "Are you checking in? Do you need help with bags or anything?"

"We're fine, but thanks," Marthe said. "Perhaps we'll see you later?"

"Possibly. I'm Will, by the way. Will Grant." He offered his hand.

"Marthe Kinney. And that's my son Brendan."
Brendan came around and shook Will's hand as well.

"You're a friend of the owner?" Marthe asked.

Will thought, was he? He wanted to be so much more.

"My folks sold her this place. I grew up here. And I've been doing the renovations."

"It's beautiful, you've done a lovely job."

"Thanks. Well, I'll let you check in. Sure I can't help you at all?" Will was looking for any excuse to see Faith again, even briefly.

"I've got them," Brendan said, grabbing his parent's bags and his duffle.

Will waved as he got in his truck and drove off, and Marthe and Brendan entered the inn. Marthe, even though not an hotelier, knew what Ciaran would look for in a potential acquisition. She knew immediately he'd like this place. There was a fire in the big stone fireplace, hot apple cider and some delicious looking caramels on a sideboard, comfortable furnishings, soothing décor. It was just lovely. And not sterile. Just rough enough around the edges that it didn't look like a chain. Homey. Nice.

They approached the front desk. A tiny woman with crazy curly hair greeted them.

"Hi there! Welcome to The Jay Feather Inn, how can I help?"

Friendly and approachable. Very nice, Marthe thought.

"Checking in. The reservation is under the name Kinney."

"I have you right here. Family room for 3 people, correct?"

"That's correct."

As Iris had Marthe fill out the registration form, Faith walked out of the office. Iris grabbed the keys and was about to come around the counter to show them to their room when Faith stopped her. Brendan had been bent over scratching Peaches and Herb's ears, as they had been rubbing up against his ankles.

"I was heading upstairs, I'll be happy to take them up. Good afternoon! I'm Faith Nicholas," she said shaking Marthe's hand. Marthe gasped.

"Are you OK?" Faith asked.

"He was right. You do look like him," Marthe whispered.

"Who?" Faith asked.

Brendan stood up to say hello and he and Faith looked at each other. They both laughed. Iris looked back and forth between them.

"Wow. You guys could be brother and sister," she said in wonder. Sure it was just a fluke, Faith showed them up the stairs, grabbing a suitcase. Their family suite had two rooms, each with a bath. Marthe was pleased with them, the beautiful white down linens, the river and mountain views, and the river stone floors in the bath. Simple, elegant and not fussy. One of the inns they'd stayed at this week had four different floral prints in a small room. It had instantly given Marthe a headache.

"What time would you like dinner?" Faith asked.

"My husband should be here shortly. Would it be a problem if I waited for him before I gave you an answer?"

"Not at all. Can I get you anything?"

"Actually, I think I'm going to go down to your beautiful great room and have a cup of cider. Your fireplace looks very inviting."

"Do you have Wi-Fi?" Brendan asked.

Faith showed him the instructions and password.

"Um, can you tell me... What time does Kendra come to work?" Brendan asked.

"Oh! Um, around five. You know her?" Faith smiled.

"Yes. We met her in town today. She said to ask for her tonight," Brendan blushed.

"I'll make sure you're at her table." Faith winked.

Marthe and Brendan made themselves comfortable in the great room. Brendan kept an eye toward the dining room for Kendra, and Marthe watched the goings on of the inn while enjoying the classical music playing softly in the background. Wonderful smells were wafting from the kitchen. Laughter could be heard in the bar. It seemed such a happy place. Marthe didn't know the overall plan CLI had for the inns they'd frequented this week, but she couldn't help but think what a shame it would be to change a thing about this one.

Patty and Jack entered the front door carrying bags of aromatic bread. The delivery truck had broken down and Faith had requested the bakery let one of her staff go to the service garage to get their order. They agreed and Jack offered to drive Patty so Faith's staff could continue to set up for dinner. Patty smiled at the woman on the sofa and she smiled back. She noticed a young man opposite, but he had his head in an iSomething. Patty took the bread to the kitchen as Jack brought the receipt to Faith at the desk.

Randy Preston gave Ciaran a ride to The Jay Feather in his personal car, as Ciaran didn't want to drive up the long drive in a limo. The conversation was sparse; Randy knew Ciaran wasn't happy with the day and Randy was a bit upset about Kim's shakiness. It was going to be a long night, as he'd need to go back to the office and help her pull the new dossiers together. So both men were lost in thought. As they pulled off the road onto The Jay Feather's drive Ciaran noticed the sign, under which sat beautiful fall flowers and hay bales, and as they approached the inn he noticed a welcoming, well lit entrance with flowers, pumpkins and corn stalks. Seasonal and charming.

"This is how an inn should look," Ciaran said quietly to himself. "Thanks for the lift. See you tomorrow," he said more loudly. Randy nodded to the boss and as Ciaran walked up the steps he drove off.

Ciaran walked in to the heavenly aromas of roasted meat and wood smoke. It brought him back to his childhood at his parent's pub. He spotted his family in front of the fire.

"Oh good, you're here!" Marthe said, putting down her book. "Be a love and tell them at the desk what time you'd like to have dinner." She kissed him. "Long day?"

"Bloody hell yes. I could use a pint. Or a whiskey. Maybe both."

"Well, your son has his eye on our waitress tonight, so be on your best behaviour."

"Met a bird, did you?" Ciaran smiled at Brendan. "Brilliant."

Brendan grinned sheepishly. Ciaran looked around for the front desk, and Marthe pointed him in the right direction.

"We'll probably get a drink at the tap, Bren. Are you alright here?" Marthe asked.

He nodded and was watching his parents walk toward the desk when he saw Kendra in the dining room. She was tying her black apron on and saw him across the inn. She waved. He stood to go speak to her.

Faith looked up from her conversation with Jack to see Marthe Kinney and who she guessed was her husband approaching. Patty came out of the kitchen and looked up at the group. The young man she'd seen before was now facing her. He looked exactly like Faith. Her heart began to race. She looked at his parents. The father turned and was facing her head on. Her heart almost stopped.

"Ciaran!" she gasped, just before she fainted.

TWENTY TWO

Jack was close enough to catch Patty before she hit the floor. He scooped her up and brought her to a sofa in the great room. Faith followed him in and shouted to Iris to bring some whiskey. Ciaran, Marthe and Brendan were close behind.

"Ciaran, how does she know your name?" Marthe asked.

Faith's head snapped up. "Ciaran... Kinney?" she asked.

"No, Lynch," Brendan offered.

"You're Ciaran Lynch?" Faith asked, as her face paled. Iris handed her the snifter, which she waved under her mom's nose. Jack was patting her hand almost hoping she'd sleep through this part. Patty's head jerked up with a start.

"Do you remember a Patty Nicholas?" Faith asked Ciaran.

Light dawned in Ciaran's eyes. He looked at her. "Patty? From Boston? I haven't heard from you since we were Brendan's age!" Patty looked up at him, tears leaking out from her eyes.

"Ciaran, we have to talk," Patty said quietly.

Marthe looked from Patty to Faith to Ciaran.

"Is this your mother?" she asked Faith.

Faith nodded. Marthe looked at Ciaran.

"Darling, I think you have a daughter," she said matter of factly to Ciaran.

"Am I the only fecking idjit doesn't know what's on here?" Ciaran shouted.

"Look at her! Look at Brendan! Look in a mirror. That is your child!"

"What!" He looked at Patty. She nodded, closing her eyes. "How could you not tell me?"

Brendan's eyes were wide as he looked at Faith. A sister. He didn't know how he felt about that. Faith was tearing up now, watching her mom cry. Iris backed out of the room, pulling Kendra with her. Jack looked at Patty and raised his eyebrows.

"I'm OK. It's OK," she said. He got up and joined Iris. She handed him the snifter of whiskey and he downed it.

112

"Keep 'em comin'," he said.

Buck, who had been sitting at the bar, stood in the doorway with his pint.

Faith rose from her mother's side and looked at her father.

"I'll let you two talk," she said.

Marthe pulled Brendan toward the stairs. She turned and looked at Ciaran.

"Darling, any other offspring I should be aware of?" She said. Ciaran looked stricken.
Marthe smiled. "By the looks of things you could have done much worse." She looked at Faith. "I won't be a wicked stepmother, I quite think we'll like each other." She and Brendan disappeared up the steps.

Faith grabbed a box of tissues from the check-in desk, put them in front of her mother and left, turning Buck around and pushing him back into the Taproom. He snickered.

Ciaran and Patty were alone. Patty didn't know where to begin.

"You just stopped writing," Ciaran said. "I finally gave up."

"We were kids. What would you have done if I'd called and said, 'Hey, I'm pregnant!'"

"I dunno." He shook his head and closed his eyes.

"I was going to put her up for adoption. My parents thought you might try to stop me, that's why they thought it was best not to tell you. But I just... couldn't let her go. And I didn't want you to think she was a burden."

"She might have been, at the beginnin'. Me folks never had much. They won't let me give them much now! They think they're born to serve. But Patty, they'd have loved to know they had a grandchild. Even if we couldn't have helped much."

Patty's tears flowed freely. "I'm so sorry. It really has made me sad that you haven't known her. She's so much like you. She even tilts her head and wiggles her fingers like you do."

"Does she?" he smiled, but his head was spinning. "Has she not ever asked about me?"

"Once. She wanted to know your name. She never asked again."

"You could have..."

"What? Had her contact you? Told her about how an innocent roll in the hay was her humble beginning? I never lied to her, Ciaran. I just never told her... anything."

Ciaran looked around. "She's done well for herself."

"She has. And your company is trying to take it away from her." Patty started to cry again. "I considered contacting you to ask you to stop... She's dreamt of a place like this her whole life. She's making a home here, one I was never able to give her. We moved so much." Patty told him who she worked for and how she made her living.

"Really?" Ciaran asked. She nodded. He got it. He understood the life of a corporate hotelier. "Then she comes by this honestly."

"Yes, she does. And she doesn't know it's your company that's trying to take her business."

"Whoa, slow down. I'd never take her business. Offer to buy it perhaps. Besides, how do you know this?" he asked.

Patty explained Kim Edgeworth's relationship with Will.

"You're a majority shareholder in the mortgage company that holds the paper here. And the fine print says you could call the note."

"We don't do that. We make great offers on the properties we buy, most owners are beggin' us to buy them."

"She doesn't want to sell. And I'm prepared to give her my life's savings so she doesn't have to."

Ciaran sat back and ran his hands through his hair.

"Of all the places I saw this week this looks like the only one I'd want to buy..."

"I know you don't even know her, but you'd break her heart. Please don't do it. Once you know her you'll love her, I know you will. Don't start off as her adversary."

"This is a lot to hear, Patty. I may just need to go get a wee bit skuddered in the pub."

114

TWENTY THREE

Marthe sat looking out the window at the lights of O'Dell down the road. The night sky was lovely and the sound of the river was peaceful. But she didn't feel at peace. She couldn't imagine what Ciaran was going through. Or how Brendan must feel finding out he has a sister. She asked him if he wanted to talk but he shook his head, went into his room and shut the door. How did she feel? A bit numb actually. Was her family was about to be turned upside down? She had no idea what to expect. Was this meeting truly accidental? Did the girl really not know who her father was? What an interesting dilemma, she thought; not knowing your own father might be attempting to purchase your new business. Would Ciaran just distance himself? Or would he want this young woman in his life? And would she want anything to do with him once she knew his plan? Usually if CLI couldn't obtain a property they wanted they'd find one nearby and become its competitor. Or might he just back off and not tell her? She really didn't know how he would play this one. He'd been different lately. Almost needy, wanting them to take this family trip together, mixing business with pleasure, actually spending time with them... She wanted to ask him what he'd done with her husband. She enjoyed her solitude, it gave her time to work on her silkscreens and manage her agent, and left time for her friends, but she could do with a bit more Ciaran time. But as the dutiful wife who wanted for nothing she was not about to complain. But this week, well, this had been grand.

Brendan came out of his room and looked around in the dark.

"Mum, are you here?"

"Yes, darling, over by the window. Shall I light a lamp?"

"No."

"How are you?" she asked.

"Dunno. Confused I guess. Is she really my sister?"

"I'm pretty certain she is. Half sister, anyway," she added.

"What happens now?" he asked.

115

"Darling, I have no idea. We'll have to take the lead from your Da," she said, but then corrected herself. "That's not entirely true. You do have a say in this. She is your sister and if you want to get to know her you have every right."

"Really?"

Marthe nodded. He could make out her profile against the window.

"I think... Well, she seems nice," Brendan said.

"Yes, she does. And she's very bright, obviously a good businesswoman. But we'll have to get to know her better."

"You don't mind?"

"Darling, why should I mind? If it will make you happy I am totally in support."

"Do you think she wants Da's money?"

"Brendan, I don't think she knows he has any. This meeting wasn't planned. And if she knew who he was and that he had money why didn't she come after him long ago?"

"Good point."

The door opened and Ciaran stood in silhouette in the doorway. Marthe reached over and turned on the lamp nearest her chair. She took a long look at her husband. He looked older than he had an hour ago. She rose and went to him, putting her arms around him. Brendan sat on their bed and watched.

"I have a daughter," he said quietly.

Patty and Faith sat on Faith's bed as Patty attempted to regain her composure.

"Faith, I'm so sorry. I should have told you more about him. I should have told him about you." The tears started again.

"Mom, it was your decision. I understand." She hugged her mother.

"Weren't you ever curious? You never asked, except for that one time."

"Of course I was. Grandpa told me everything."

"WHAT!"

"When I turned 15. He said I should know about my father. He told me he was Irish, and that his family owned a pub. That you met him on a school trip, and that you... hmm, I think he said, 'cared about him deeply, but were both so

116

young and far apart that it wasn't fair to burden him with a baby at such a young age'. He even told me they wanted you to give me up for adoption, but once you saw me you wouldn't. And he said that when they saw me they agreed. So I knew I could always go looking for him, but I didn't need to. I had you, and Grandpa and Gram. It's not like he knew I existed and took off. I didn't hate him or anything, I just had everything I could possibly want."

Patty looked at her with her mouth open.

"Did you ever even Google him?" she asked.

"No. I wasn't really curious. What good could it do? I'd bust his world apart. Sort of like tonight."

"What are you going to do now? Do you want to know him?"

"I guess that's up to him. It's sort of cool having a baby brother, though."

"I can't believe how much alike the two of you look."

"I know!"

Faith heard Hank whining and then there was a knock on the door. Will stuck his head in and Hank pushed the door wide and trotted over to Faith demanding her attention. She laughed. Hank was still in love with her even if Will wasn't.

"Um, sorry to interrupt, but Jack filled me in. I was just checking to see if you're OK."

Faith looked at him and felt her heart fill. Even apart he looked after her.

"I'm fine. Mom's a bit of a mess, though." Faith crashed her shoulder against her mom's, grinning.

"I totally understand," Will said. "Can I get you ladies anything? Adult beverages? Tea?"

"You're a sweetheart, Will," Patty said, "but no thanks. We'll be out in a minute."

"By the way, Hank called it." Will said. Hank was half in Faith's lap and she was nuzzling his head.

"What do you mean," she asked.

"When they pulled up in front Hank went right to Brendan and did all the stuff he does when he sees you."

"Really?" Faith kissed the dog's head. "You're a smart boy, aren't you? Let's go." She stood and put her hand out for her mother. Patty grabbed it and stood, wrapping her daughter in a hug.

"I'm not kissing you, though, you just kissed the dog."

Jack was sitting at the bar when they emerged, but Buck had disappeared. Kendra was waiting tables in the dining room; it was a quiet night with only a few inn guests, and the Lynch party had not come down from their rooms. Faith looked at Iris behind the bar. Her eyes were wide, not knowing what to do or expect. Faith chuckled.

"Iris, it's OK. We're all fine. The world isn't ending anytime soon. At least for me," Faith said. Iris visibly relaxed. "Any sign of them?"

Iris and Jack both shook their heads. Patty joined Jack at the bar.

"Iris, I'd like a Stoli Martini straight up. Extra cold, extra olives," Patty said.

"Yes, ma'am!"

Patty grabbed Jack's hand and held it to her chest. He touched her face with his free hand, caressing her cheek. His look was imploring.

"I'm fine, too. I guess I always wondered if this shoe was ever going to drop," she said. He nodded.

Will put his hand gently on Faith's shoulder. He was hiding his feelings from the world when all he wanted tonight was to let Faith know he was there for her.

"What are you going to do?" he asked her. She turned her head and smiled sadly.

"I'm going to go and take care of my guests."

Faith walked up the stairs with a tray. It held a bottle of Whistle Pig whiskey, three glasses, ice, and a bottle of local root beer. She knocked on the door. Brendan answered. He looked at her as if he was surprised to see her. She looked past him and saw Marthe and Ciaran Lynch on the settee. Brendan stepped aside.

"May I come in?" she asked. Ciaran stood. "I thought perhaps you could use this," she said.

Ciaran surveyed the tray.

"Will you be joining us?" he asked.

"If you'll let me."

"Come in," he said.

She put the tray on the table and handed Brendan the root beer.

"Is that OK? I have other stuff if you'd prefer…"

"No, this is good, really!"

Faith looked at Marthe and Ciaran.

"Ice? This drinks hot, just so you know." Marthe nodded, Ciaran shook his head. Faith poured the drinks and handed them out.

"Slàinte," Faith and Ciaran said at the same time. They smiled shyly at each other.

"The apple doesn't fall far from the tree," Marthe quipped. "Faith, please sit down."

She sat in an armchair as Brendan and Ciaran went back to their seats.

"So what happens now?" Ciaran asked.

"I guess that's up to you. We can't un-know any of this. I just want you to understand that I don't want anything from you. Nothing material, anyway. But now that you know about me I wouldn't mind knowing you. And Brendan."

Brendan's eyes lit up.

"I have no idea what to call you," Faith smiled at Ciaran sadly.

"Da, of course," Brendan said immediately. Faith laughed.

"Wow, that's Irish." She looked to her father. "Are you OK with that?"

He'd taken a sip of the whiskey and was sitting back observing her, watching her and Brendan next to each other, seeing how they'd have been mistaken for twins had they been closer in age. He smiled and nodded.

"Faith is a beautiful name," he said. "A beautiful name for a beautiful girl."

Faith blushed.

"Tell me about yourself, lass. I want to know what I missed," Ciaran said.

"Um, that could take some time. I know this has all been a shock, but what I know of teenage boys that stay here is that they're always hungry. Would you like to come down and join me for dinner?"

"Can we dine with everyone?" Marthe asked. "I'd like to get to know your mother."

"Uh, sure, I'm sure that would be fine. Just be warned that when I left the bar Iris had just made her a Martini she could bathe in."

"Understandable," Marthe replied. She tossed back the rest of her drink. "Now we're even."

TWENTY FOUR

When Randy got back to the office Kim was gone. He tried her cell phone and got voice mail. He paced the office, close to panic. How was he going to get this presentation ready for tomorrow when the files were all on her computer? He went through her desk looking for hard copies, a flash drive or a CD that might have the data. What he found alarmed him. She had vials of medication dated months ago that had not been touched. She had notes about The Jay Feather Inn with details about their business she would never have had access to. And he found scribbled pages of alarming threats Kim had written to Faith Nicholas, The Jay Feather's owner, but had never sent. He looked at the medication vials. They were for the same drug. He opened his laptop and Googled the name of the drug. Anti-psychotic? And she hadn't taken it? He wasn't sure what that meant for her, exactly, but he thought it probably wasn't good.

Kim stood naked in front of the bathroom mirror. She needed a shower after the day she'd had. So much had gone wrong, and she knew she needed to go back to the office to complete the new dossiers for the meeting tomorrow, but she wanted a break. Just a short one. And she received a text telling her to go home.

He entered the cottage and slipped down the hall, he could see the light in the bathroom. He stepped in and she looked at him in the mirror. She looked down. He walked up behind her and stared into her eyes as he unzipped his pants. He pushed her legs apart and entered her slowly. She moaned and closed her eyes. He reached around and fondled her breasts as he pushed against her, watching her face in the mirror. He grabbed her hips and started to work her harder. He could feel himself getting close as she began to pant and moan, and he felt her spasms as he rocked her, and he groaned his pleasure as he came. Before she'd even caught her breath he leaned down over her and whispered in her ear.

"Stop pretending you don't like it."

Kim's head shot up and looked at him in the mirror, her face shocked. He smiled, zipped his pants, and left.

Randy Preston wasn't sure what to do. He reached out for the doctor listed on the prescription vials, and was told that unless he was a health care proxy listed by the patient the doctor could give him no information. HIPAA rules, you see. Unsure what to do now he took a chance and called a friend of his younger brother's from Waterbury who he knew had gone to med school. They'd lost touch, but the Internet always provided and he'd found his brother's friend in minutes. And not only was he a doctor, he was also a shrink. The receptionist paged the doctor and connected the call.

"Dr. Gregson here," he answered.

"Sandy? Randy Preston. Shawn's brother."

"Randy! Talk about a blast from the past!"

"I know, I know. Listen, I'm really sorry to bother you with this but I think I might have an emergency situation here and I don't know what to do." Randy went on to explain the vials of pills, the threatening letters and the erratic behavior. He also mentioned his inability to get anywhere with the doctor of record.

"I know who that is, and he practices in Maryland!" Sandy said. "The guys a genius at pharmapsychology, but patients should be closely monitored. Hard to do that from 600 miles away."

"Sandy, what do I do?"

"I hate to say this, but there isn't much you can do. Unless she tries to hurt herself or someone else, or clearly has a psychotic break and needs hospitalization you can't force her to do anything. And you need to tread lightly here. Any big upset could push her over the edge. Did the doctor say he'd at least call and check on her?"

"I never got past the receptionist."

"Well, give me her name. I'll call her doctor and see if I can get him to follow up with her."

"Kim Edgeworth."

"Seriously?" Sandy was alarmed.

"Yuh. Why?"

"She's the reason I became a shrink!" He was sorry the words had left his lips. "She's not my patient but to be respectful of her privacy I can't give you details."

121

"But it's that bad?"

There was silence on the line.

"Can you at least come and talk to her?" Randy asked.

"Let me track down her doctor and I'll get back to you."

Kim dressed and stood in her kitchen in the dark. She was confused. She needed to get back to work. She had to think. What had just happened? No, stop, focus on the problem. She needed to get the property away from her. And if she couldn't get The Jay Feather for CLI this whole project would fall through. She'd be demoted at least, or fired at worst. And worst still Will would choose Faith, not Kim. What could she use as leverage? What would bring Faith Nicholas to her knees? What had she learned about her that she could use? He'd been bringing her information, there had to be something.

The Jay Feather's projections were far above those on her original business plan. How could she hurt the business and turn those numbers to dust? The Christmas Festival! Dan Churchill had come to Kim looking for sponsorship of the festival, or at least an ad for The Overlook. Kim was sure CLI would own The Jay Feather Inn by the time of the festival, so she signed CLI up as THE major sponsor, and put an ad in for The Overlook as well. That bill hadn't been paid yet. If she pulled the sponsorship the O'Dell Christmas Festival would collapse. No festival, no occupancy, and the three weeks around the festival The Jay Feather Inn was completely sold out. Those dollars would have held the inn until ski season, and without them she might default on her loan.

Could she spin it so it looked like Faith was the reason the festival was cancelled? She could write a press release saying Faith's reluctance to sell to CLI caused them to rethink the sponsorship. It would be all her fault. She'd be a pariah. They'd all hate her.

But what would Ciaran Lynch do? Kim knew he'd thank her for following through on the plan. She knew it.

Sandy Gregson contacted Kim Edgeworth's doctor, John Roth, in Maryland, who, as a professional courtesy, agreed to speak with him. Sandy explained the situation.

"She's cancelled her last two appointments with me." Dr. Roth explained. "I have spoken with her personally and she seemed to be doing well, but you know how that goes."

"Yes, of course," Sandy replied. "They don't want you to stop them from cutting back on their meds so they are careful to answer correctly…"

"And without blood work I couldn't be sure. She hasn't had her blood taken recently," Dr. Roth added. "I'll try to contact her."

"Can I be of any assistance?" Sandy asked. "I actually knew her in high school."

"Perhaps. May I contact you after I've spoken with her?"

"Of course."

They said their goodbyes and hung up.

Sandy called Randy Preston.

"Her doctor is reaching out for her. If he needs me to get involved he'll let me know. I'm guessing he'll probably call whoever is her emergency contact and ask them to intervene," Sandy relayed.

"I thought of that. It's her father; I looked up her personnel file. But he's in Maryland."

"Lets hope she keeps it together until he arrives."

TWENTY FIVE

Faith went to the dining room to have Kendra set a table for the Lynches and to prepare her mom for this evening. She looked around. Patty and Jack were at the bar but Will was gone.

"Probably best," she thought. *"I have enough to navigate tonight."*

Jack and Patty looked at her expectantly.

"Mom, they'd like to have dinner with us."

Patty hung her head. "I guess I should have skipped the martini."

"Or had a second," Jack added.

"I think it'll be fine. Jack? Will you join us?" Faith asked.

"I don't think it's my place."

"Please?" Patty asked quietly as she squeezed his hand.

"Really?" he asked. She nodded.

"Good." Faith headed off efficiently, flagging Kendra and Iris to set up a table and then heading to the kitchen to tell Delroy what to cook.

"Ya, mon. You got a whole heap a drama in de house tonight!" Delroy exclaimed when he saw her. "You irie boss lady?"

"I'm OK, Delroy. But I need you to outdo yourself tonight, my friend." She told him what she wanted.

"Me mash it up, boss lady."

The Lynches entered the dining room to find Kendra smiling a welcome and showing them to their table. Patty, Jack and Faith were waiting for them there. Faith introduced Jack to her new family and Ciaran introduced his wife and son to Patty. There was tension, but Faith could also feel excitement. They sat and Kendra took their beverage orders.

"I hope you don't mind, I've asked Chef to prepare a special dinner so we could have time to talk and not have to be bothered with menus," Faith said. "Any food allergies or dislikes?"

"None," Ciaran said. "We eat everything."

"Great."

"So, Patty, tell me what you do," Marthe asked.

And they were off. The conversation went nonstop through five courses, with everything from education to travel, food, and family history. Mostly it was Ciaran and Marthe asking questions of Faith and Patty, with Brendan behaving as Faith predicted and wolfing down every course put before him. And Kendra bringing him extras of the things he really liked. He particularly liked Faith's country style paté, butternut squash ravioli and veal tournedos with sage brown butter, but he was equally happy with the wild mushroom soup and fennel salad. But his favorite was the flourless chocolate cake. He had two huge pieces, which Kendra cut herself.

They moved into the great room and sat in front of the fire with coffee and after dinner drinks. The conversation had gone long into the evening, past the departures of other diners and long after the other inn guests had retired to their rooms.

Finally the topic Patty had feared came to light.

"Lass, I have something I need to tell you," Ciaran started. Faith looked concerned and Patty held her breath. "I haven't spoken about me self much, but it will soon come to light that I am the President and CEO of CLI, which stands for Ciaran Lynch International."

Faith swallowed hard. She looked pained.

"I had no idea who you were," he continued. "And I don't know what you've heard but I'm not a monster. Yes, I buy up troubled properties if there's a good business reason to do it. And we'll buy a profitable place at a good price if it fits our portfolio..."

"But the bank you have majority shares in... Worldwide Mortgage. My mortgage is there. There's language that says you can call the note..." Faith interrupted.

"Mm. Yes there is, and I'll tell you why. For a while about ten years ago we tried franchising some of our properties. You're in the business, you know how it works, but for Jack's sake I'll explain." Jack nodded his thanks. "Instead of running these properties ourselves we allowed them to be franchised by management companies who leased our branding. We still have a few successful franchisers out there, but some of them failed. We put the language in the contract specifically so we could force a franchiser out of a

125

property before too much damage was done to the property, or our brand, in the event they were not good hoteliers. Then we'd take the property back and install our own team to turn it around. It would continue to be a corporate hotel and not be refranchised at that point. So the language has remained in all of the contracts for that reason. I've never forced a hostile takeover of a successful business, or for that matter a business that wasn't a franchise we'd sold. I've offered big money to buy flourishing businesses, and a majority of the time been successful, but I've also walked away from some who weren't willing to sell."

Faith listened carefully.

"Lass, I've no intention of taking this away from you." Ciaran reached over and took her hand while gesturing with the other. "But I'd like to talk to you about your business."

"You wouldn't try to compete with her in her own market?" Patty looked concerned.

"No. I'd like to discuss having a small consortium of inns, all as beautiful and well run as The Jay Feather, with you at the helm. They'd be local so you'd not have to travel more than 100 miles or so, and The Jay Feather would be the flagship."

"Economies of scale..." Faith said, lost in thought. "How many?" she asked, her brow furrowed.

"Six or so?" He said. "You'd have complete control over renovations, design, food."

"Faith, Sweetie, you just got here. Do you want to make a major change like this so soon? And you'd be working for a corporation again..." Patty added.

"Not necessarily," Ciaran interrupted. "It could be a joint venture, a subsidiary of CLI. We'd be equal shareholders."

"I don't have that kind of money," Faith whispered, shaking her head.

"I do. Lass, I didn't know you existed before tonight. I have thirty years of child support to pay." He smiled.

"This is so fast. Are you sure you want to do this? Don't you even want a paternity test?" Faith asked.

Marthe laughed. "Darling, there's no doubt in my mind that you are his daughter, no test is required." She'd been observing Faith all evening. There was so much of Ciaran in her; there would be no denying this child.

"And you're OK with this?" Faith asked Marthe.

"It's the right thing to do," she replied.

"Think about it. Sleep on it. No response is required tonight," Ciaran said, patting her hand.

"Thanks... Da." Faith said tentatively. Ciaran smiled.

TWENTY SIX

Kim's phone buzzed. Her screen identified the caller as Dr. Roth. His office was the last call she wanted to receive, so she hit ignore. Her head was spinning. She had that feeling again. No, stop it. She pulled into the parking lot of The Overlook and looked up at the night sky. It was getting colder, and the last leaves on the trees were falling fast. The wind picked them up and blew them around, making her dizzy.

She walked into her office to find Randy at her desk, working on his computer. She braced herself, for she knew he'd be angry that she was gone for so long considering how much work they'd have to do tonight to get back on track for tomorrow. It had taken her a while to contact Dan Churchill, and when she'd pulled both the sponsorship and the ad he'd tried vehemently to talk her out of it. He'd even told her the festival would be cancelled, as he'd not be able to pay for all the infrastructure and personnel needs as required by the state. Never mind the supplies or the permits. She feigned sympathy but said the decision was made over her head and there was nothing she could do. But it took a while to get him to shut up. Then she had to write and e-mail the press release telling the world CLI was pulling out and The O'Dell Christmas Festival would be cancelled. She made sure Faith was blamed. She wrote "Because of a conflict of interest with the owner of The Jay Feather Inn, CLI has been forced to withdraw its support from this worthwhile event." CLI wouldn't shoulder any blame and Faith would look like a monster.

Kim attempted normalcy with Randy, but she could feel something happening, a panicky feeling in her chest. The thing that happened before... She pushed that thought far away, sent it as deep as she could.

"Hi Randy, I needed to take care of some other business, sorry it took so long." Her eyes darted nervously. Were they here, the ones that bothered her?

"No problem, Kim. You're back now, that's all that matters." He smiled brightly at her. He wondered what was going on. She looked haunted. "Do you have those files?" he asked.

"Yes, right here."

Randy took the folders and quickly reviewed them. He was having a hard time concentrating, afraid of what Kim might do. He just wanted her father to get here and deal with this. He saw in the files that these inns would need a lot of capital improvements and that he'd probably over-promised on these properties to Ciaran Lynch. He got angry and it showed in his face. Kim saw his look and panicked.

Kim started to talk about the properties. She confused three of them, referred to two by the wrong names, and mentioned how one was perfect as it was, which was not the case. She had them mixed up with those presented earlier today. Her phone buzzed again. She looked down to see her doctor's name on caller ID again.

"No, no, no," she started to repeat. She took the phone and threw it against the wall. Randy stood up.

"Kim, are you okay?" He was nervous, not sure what was going to happen.

"She can't win, she can't have him," she began muttering under her breath. Randy approached her and tried to take her arms and lead her to a chair. "Get away from me!" she shrieked. "You're just like them! Just like them! You won't leave me alone. Why won't they leave me alone?" Kim collapsed to the floor. Randy called security and asked they call an ambulance and send someone to the office to help him. She was rocking back and forth on the floor, holding herself. She looked like she'd stay put so he called Sandy Gregson's direct line. He explained the situation.

"I'm on call tonight," Sandy said. "I'll meet the ambulance at the hospital."

Peter Edgeworth was at the Burlington airport's rental car desk when his phone rang.

"Peter Edgeworth," he answered.

"Mr. Edgeworth, this is Dr. Roth, Kim's psychiatrist."

"Yes, Dr. Roth. What can I do for you?" He expected the worst.

Dr. Roth explained that Dr. Sandy Gregson had contacted him after Dr. Gregson had admitted Kim to the psych ward post evaluation. Blood work showed she had almost none of her prescribed medication in her system. Her behavior suggested she was close to or had experienced a psychotic break. She was sedated and Sandy wanted her doctor of record to weigh in on next steps. And to contact her next of kin, which is why Dr. Roth was calling Peter Edgeworth. Dr. Roth suggested Mr. Edgeworth get to Vermont as soon as he was able.

"Dr. Roth, I'm already here. Another concerned party contacted me to tell me about my daughter's recent behavior, suggesting she was close to relapse. I was planning to call you once I'd actually seen her for myself. It sounds like I'm already too late."

"Mr. Edgeworth, once Kim is stabilized and back on her medical regimen there can be great improvement. Please don't give up hope. I've spoken with Dr. Gregson. I believe you will find she is in good hands. And I'm available for consultation any time Dr. Gregson needs me."

Peter Edgeworth thanked the doctor, ended the call and silently shook his head.

His drive to the hospital was fraught with random thoughts. What if she can't be stabilized this time? What happens next? He felt as though a lead blanket had been laid on his chest. He thought of everything and nothing, all at once.

By the time he got to the hospital Kim was asleep. Not the peaceful, dreaming slumber he remembered from when she was a child but a troubled, fitful sleep. She was anchored to the hospital bed by soft restraints. All of the horror came flooding back to him, the disbelief, the shock of the diagnosis, the wretched girl his daughter was turned into by her mental illness, and once stabilized, the eventual acceptance of what would become her new normal. A woman measured and evened by her drugs, without the highs and lows. She'd need psychiatric care her whole life. She'd need these terrible medications; the lifesaving but side-effect inducing medicine that would make her life livable and miserable at the same time. She didn't want to saddle another with her baggage, so she'd shied away from relationships. And she could never risk getting pregnant because the drugs would affect the child, so she felt less than a woman, or so she had told her mom.

But she'd done so well for the last dozen years. It took time to stabilize her, and she'd been hospitalized a couple of times, but once she was stable and consistently monitored she'd done well. Thrived even. She'd finished college, and got a good job. Peter had felt so proud and happy for her. So what triggered this? Was it being back here?

Sandy Gregson stood in the doorway watching Mr. Edgeworth and his daughter. Sandy had seen this sight many times before, a parent distraught by their child's illness. Not an illness an antibiotic would cure, or an operation would fix, but a life-long struggle for normalcy. He cleared his throat. Peter Edgeworth looked up.

"Mr. Edgeworth?" Sandy asked. Peter nodded. "Dr. Gregson." Sandy put his hand out and Peter shook it. "I'm glad you've come."

Sandy brought him up to speed on Kim's blood work, and the circumstances, as he knew them, prior to her admittance. Peter asked the hard question.

"What could have caused this?" he asked.

"From what we can tell she'd cut her medication back to almost nothing. She may have started to cut back just a bit, and then felt good, you know, started experiencing the emotions that the drugs can deaden, and didn't want to go back again so she cut back some more. It's actually pretty common."

"Might there have been a trigger?"

"Possibly. It would help if I knew the circumstances around her initial breakdown. But lets talk elsewhere, not here."

Peter kissed Kim on the forehead and followed Sandy out of the room. Sandy led Peter down the hall to a conference room, stopping to get them each a cup of coffee on the way in. They sat down. Peter looked haggard. Sandy knew this wasn't going to be pleasant for him.

"This falls under doctor-patient confidentiality, right?" Peter asked.

"Of course," Sandy said, nodding. "I know a little of the history. I'm a friend of Will Grant's."

"Ah, I see. Good. I won't have to tell you about their relationship and the horrible things she did to him."

"Correct."

"Well, here's the part nobody knows. Her mom and I didn't even know until we moved to Maryland and she started intensive counseling after she was stabilized. Kim was raped while we lived in O'Dell."

Sandy hung his head. "I'm so sorry, Mr. Edgeworth." Sandy wasn't sure if he wanted to know by whom, so he just let the man talk.

"She," he paused, "she wouldn't tell us who it was, so we could never press charges. But she swore it wasn't Will. She said that she and Will hadn't even been intimate, they were waiting to get married."

Sandy relaxed inwardly. He couldn't imagine Will being violent, and based on what a stand-up guy Will was Sandy could see him respecting her wishes about sex before marriage.

"Mr. Edgeworth, it's not uncommon for a psychotic break to be brought on from a violent act."

"I know that now. But there's more. Kim was pregnant. She didn't know it, but it was verified at the hospital."

"Did she have the child?" Sandy asked.

"No. She miscarried. Possibly because of the medications, although no one has ever said for sure. She took it very hard. She didn't want to bear the child, but she understood that because of her medications she wouldn't be able to have children. Something changed in her then. She seemed resigned to her situation. Numb, almost. She was never the same."

"Have there been any relationships since?" Sandy asked.

"A couple. Nothing lasting. She was so afraid of letting anyone in, and so afraid of another pregnancy that she steered clear. And I don't think she trusted many men."

Sandy thought for a moment. Here Kim was, back in the O'Dell area. Was that enough to trigger a relapse or was it strictly her lapse in medication. Or had she re-experienced her trigger?

"Mr. Edgeworth, I need to ask you something. This is very difficult... Would you give permission for a rape kit to be processed on Kim? I'm wondering if her relapse was caused by her return to the area, the lack of drugs in her system, or possibly the reoccurrence of the original event. Her therapy going forward might be easier if we knew for sure."

Peter Edgeworth sat back and ran his hands through his hair. He sighed deeply.

"Can it be done in such a way that she won't know? Can she be unconscious? I don't want her to be subject to what might feel like an assault." He looked like he might cry.

"Yes. She won't remember a thing. It is very quick and painless. I promise."

Mr. Edgeworth nodded his consent.

"There's something else I should tell you," Peter said. "It was Will who called me to tell me Kim was acting erratically. He didn't want to tell me how, at first, but I finally got him to tell me she'd been texting him about sexual encounters they'd supposedly had. He swore to me he hadn't had any relations with her, and had seen her only twice since she moved here, once at The Overlook and once in O'Dell, but she'd texted him a dozen times and he didn't know what to do. He said he was in love with someone else and wanted Kim to stop. He felt like he was being stalked. But he didn't want to upset Kim. He said he'd broken off his relationship with this other woman because he was afraid Kim might try to harm her. Her texts were sexually explicit stuff, and threats against Will's new girlfriend. He called me first, because he didn't want to get the sheriff involved."

Sandy closed his eyes.

"Mr. Edgeworth, do you have any suspicions about who might have raped Kim all those years ago?"

"I do." He paused. "Will's foster brother, Rex Buckley. I guess you'd know him as Buck."

TWENTY SEVEN

The weather was turning colder. Jack had a down vest on this morning and shivered a bit as he made his way to the office. It had been late when he'd left the inn last night, and Patty looked worn out, so he kissed her goodbye and went home alone. He knew she would sleep soundly with the weight she'd been carrying lifted from her shoulders, and he knew she'd want to talk with Faith at length this morning about Ciaran Lynch's offer. He'd missed her, though, missed her body being folded into his as they slept.

Jack fired up the wood stove in the corner and flipped the sign on his door to open. He started a pot of coffee and sat down at his computer to see what news articles, press releases and other e-mails had come in overnight. He scanned the titles, and stopped short.

O'Dell Christmas Festival Cancelled For Lack Of Funding

He opened the press release and read it quickly. He reached for the phone and saw his message light blinking. He retrieved a message from Dan Churchill from the night before; he sounded frantic.

"Jack, it's Dan Churchill. Call me immediately. I'm in a jam here, buddy, and I need some advice."

The next one was from his friend Stan at *The Burlington Free Press* wanting to know if Jack had any more information on the festival's cancelation. Ditto Frank from *The Barre-Montpelier Times Argus*.

Jack weighed his options. He called The Jay Feather.

"Good morning, The Jay Feather Inn. How may I help you?" It was Iris.

"Iris, it's Jack. Hey, has Ciaran Lynch left the inn yet?"

"No, he's having coffee in the great room with Faith. Shall I get him?"

"Please."

Iris took the portable phone to Ciaran.

"Mr. Lynch, it's Jack Kimball for you."

Ciaran looked puzzled. He took the phone.

"Good Mornin' Jack."

"Maybe, maybe not," Jack said. "Something came through my e-mail this morning and I have verification from other area newspapers that they received it as well. Let me read it to you." Jack relayed the information in the release. "Ciaran, I don't know if you're aware but the festival affects the livelihood of most everyone in O'Dell, and this year especially Faith's. There was no 'conflict of interest' between Faith and The Overlook that I'm aware of. Also, the festival is a major fundraiser for The Children's Refuge, a shelter in Burlington. This is a big deal."

"Jack, I knew nothing about this, neither the sponsorship nor the festival, not a bloody thing. Let me call the office and find out how this got all bloody bollixed up. I'll ring ye back."

"Trouble?" Faith asked.

"As Jack just said, 'maybe, maybe not'. Excuse me, darlin', I need to make a call."

Randy was at Kim's desk, trying his best to pull something together for Ciaran. He didn't want to have to explain last night to his boss. How had Kim gotten hired, for Christ's sake? Don't we do background checks? His cell phone rang. Crap, it was Ciaran.

"Good morning, sir."

"Randy, do you know anything about The O'Dell Christmas Festival?" he asked.

"Uh, no, I'm afraid I don't."

"Well, here's the thing..."

Ciaran repeated the highlights of the press release to Randy. He mentioned Kim Edgeworth had sent it last evening. Perhaps he could ask her about it. Randy hung his head.

"Well, sir, actually I can't." Randy relayed the events of last evening to Ciaran, and what little he knew of Kim's history. Before Ciaran could respond Randy began to rant about their hiring policy and how he would personally see to it that it was changed...

"Jaysus, lad! Calm yourself. The poor girl's in hospital, have some compassion. She's done a good job for us over the years, has she not?"

"Um, yes sir. She has."

"Then she was a good hire. Everyone has their lot in life and this is hers. No one is getting fired today."

"Yes sir."

"Now, can you retract that press release and get this festival back on track?"

After swigging back three cups of coffee Jack heard from Ciaran, and he immediately called Dan Churchill.

"Dan, it's Jack. The press release is being retracted and your funding is being reinstated," he said.

"It may be too late," Dan said sadly.

"Why?"

"The deadline for permits was this morning as nine. If I'd submitted them with the fees and defaulted I'd have lost all the money. So I didn't submit them. I have to pay all the deposits back to all the vendors, I couldn't risk losing their funds."

"Seriously? A couple of hours? The state can't be that rigid."

"They aren't. The actual deadline was two weeks ago, but they cut me a break because the vendors are usually waiting for the proceeds from the harvest festivals they do in October to pay our fees. I'm actually two weeks late."

"Dammit."

"Got any friends in high places?" Dan asked.

"Lemme call you back."

TWENTY EIGHT

Sandy read the report and pursed his lips. How was he going to explain this to Kim's father? He walked to her room and found Peter Edgeworth dozing in the chair, holding his daughter's hand. He'd obviously spent the night.

The sun streamed in the window and across Kim's face. Sandy had forgotten how lovely she was. He checked Kim's monitors and pulse rate, doing what he could to avoid waking her father. He considered coming back later. Peter stirred and opened his eyes.

"Lets talk," Sandy said quietly.

They got coffee and went back to the conference room.

"Mr. Edgeworth, I have the results from the rape kit."

"And...?"

Sandy paused.

"It showed evidence of sexual activity, as recent as yesterday. But not rape. Whatever activity there was it was consensual. There was semen found as well; no condom was used."

"Dear God. Please tell me she's not pregnant!"

"Not at this time. Her blood test was normal."

"But who?"

"Perhaps someone at work might know?" Sandy suggested.

"Could it have been Will? He told me it wasn't him. But it was consensual. Who else?"

Sandy didn't want to see Will dragged into this, but there was only one way to prove it wasn't him.

"Mr. Edgeworth, contact Will and tell him what's happened. He'll either fess up or be willing to submit to a DNA test. Then you'll know for sure."

"And then what? She had a lover, either Will or someone else. So what?"

"Or she submitted to someone stronger than her who knew he could take advantage of her. Perhaps her rapist of all of those years ago. If Kim was hearing voices and becoming delusional... well, let me just say that her relationship with her rapist may be... complicated."

137

Will was on his way from the lumberyard to the inn when his phone rang. He saw Peter Edgeworth's number and pulled the truck off the road. Will wasn't sure what to expect.

"Will Grant," he answered.

"Peter Edgeworth here, Will. I need to talk to you, is there somewhere we can meet?"

They pulled into town at the same time and met at The Buttery Scone. Kendra was out of school this week as Thanksgiving was Thursday, and she was picking up as many shifts as she could. She poured them both coffee and looked at them expectantly.

"Thank you, Kendra. I think that's all." Will smiled at her. She smiled back and walked away. She didn't know the man he was with.

Peter Edgeworth explained Kim's hospitalization to Will.

"I called you too late. I'm so sorry Mr. E.," Will whispered.

"There's more." He wasn't sure he was going to, but in the end he explained about the rape. How could he ask Will to submit DNA without telling him the whole story? "Will, I want to believe you when you tell me you haven't had relations with Kim, but the only way for sure is through a DNA test."

"Yeah, sure. I'll give you whatever you need. But what difference is it going to make? Couldn't she just have had a boyfriend?" Will asked.

Peter was relieved Will had consented. Now he knew for sure it wasn't him.

"The doctors think the reason she might have been texting you was she really believed the two of you were involved. And that maybe her rapist was the one she was having sex with. But we're not sure she'll be able to tell us what really happened." Peter Edgeworth looked as disturbed as he felt.

Will accompanied Peter Edgeworth to the hospital. Sandy met them and escorted Will to the lab, where the inside of his mouth was swabbed.

"You know this is crazy, right?" Will asked Sandy.

"Yup, but you're doing it to give her old man some piece of mind. He's in a bad place."

"Is Kim awake?" Will asked. Sandy shook his head.

"You know I can't tell you anything."

"Sorry. It's just..."

"I know."

Peter Edgeworth met Will outside the lab and walked him to the hospital entrance while Sandy went to check on his patient.

What Sandy couldn't share with Will was that every time Kim's sedation wore off they checked to see how she reacted, as the anti psychotic medication had to be ramped up in her system. Instead of allowing her to rant and her blood pressure to rise Sandy and Dr. Roth had agreed the best course of action was to keep her sedated until she was calmer. He entered Kim's room to find her awake but looking gaunt and sullen.

"Hello Kim. How do you feel?" he asked.

"Numb. I feel numb."

The injection he'd given her was faster acting than her previous medication, and might have fewer side effects as well. But until a manageable level could be reached she might feel over medicated.

"Do you know where you are?" he asked.

"No."

"You're in the hospital. You had an episode last night."

She looked around.

"What happened?" she asked.

"Do you remember anything?" he asked.

She thought for a moment.

"I need to go. I'm supposed to meet Will tonight. He'll be coming to my place, I can't be late." She began to pull on her restraints.

"Kim, are you hungry? Do you want to eat anything?" The distraction worked, she stopped pulling. She nodded.

Sandy went to the nurse's station and gave them instructions, and then went to find Peter Edgeworth.

Peter was thanking Will and saying goodbye to him when he saw Sandy trotting toward him from the elevator. Will stopped and waited with Peter.

"Is she all right?" Peter asked.

"Yes, she's actually lucid right now, and the nurses are going to try to feed her. But she said something..." Sandy looked at Will.

"I should go," Will said.

"No," Peter said. "It's okay, doctor, you can speak to me in front of Will."

"Kim said she was supposed to meet Will tonight."

Will shook his head sadly.

"Will, I know it's not you she's meeting. Hell, buddy, you wouldn't have been so quick to give up your DNA if there was a chance it was you. But this might be the way to find out who."

"You mean wait for him and find out who shows up?" Will asked. Sandy nodded.

TWENTY NINE

Jack and Dan had spent the day on the phone, working their way up the political ladder, trying to find someone who could help them out with their dilemma. Neither was having an easy time of it. Dan had reached out to Will for his help as he was also on the committee but his phone kept going straight to voice mail.

By early afternoon word had spread through town that the festival would be cancelled, so along with outgoing calls to anyone they thought could help Jack and Dan were fending off irate vendors and shop owners whose incomes would be hurt by the cancellation. It was a hellish day.

At five o'clock Jack and Dan decided to meet at the inn to debrief and talk about next steps. Returning funds to vendors and notifying the media that the festival was really cancelled was going to make for even more unhappy people. And Christmas was going to be a hard one, not only in O'Dell, but at The Children's Refuge, as the proceeds from the festival bought toys and Christmas dinner, and paid a good bit of the heating bill for the winter.

After Ciaran had spoken to Randy Preston he realized it was no good going to the office, and decided to spend the day getting to know his daughter and learning more about her management style. So when Jack and Dan entered the bar looking like they had come from the wars Ciaran was there to meet them.

"Lads, you look like hammered shite," he said.

Jack filled him in. Dan threw in a few more details.

"Mr. Lynch, the festival is really run on a shoestring so we can donate as much as we can to charity. We never have funds up front, so when CLI pulled out I didn't have a choice but to cancel."

Ciaran sat deep in thought, rubbing his chin.

"Whose the senator I keep readin' about, trying to stop the big box stores and start a solar farm up here somewhere?" he asked.

"Nelson Isaacs?" Jack asked.

"He's the one. Find me a phone number for him."

Jack had been calling senator's offices all day, so he pulled out a folder and read Ciaran the number, which Ciaran punched into his cell phone. Then he got up and walked into the library. Jack and Dan looked at each other and shrugged.

Patty was behind the bar. She poured Jack's scotch and Dan's draft without being asked. They both took deep swallows. Buck was at the end of the bar, nursing a beer.

"So the festival's off?" Buck said, looking sideways down the bar.

"As of right now…" Jack replied.

Faith was coming from the kitchen with Delroy's peanut butter and soy sauce popcorn, which was a hit every time it was served. She overheard the conversation.

"What?" she asked, stopping dead in her tracks. "Really? It can't be! I think all of my reservations are for the festival. And I'll need to cancel all the supplies for the soup… That's going to kill my cash flow…" she said, mostly to herself.

"Don't get ye knickers in a twist, lass," Ciaran said walking back into the room. "Danny boy, check your e-mail at half five. Should be a confirmation of all your permits for the festival. You're back in business."

"How…?" Dan looked incredulous.

"I gave Senator Isaacs his wind farm."

Everyone cheered and hugged each other as Buck quietly slipped away.

THIRTY

Peter Edgeworth managed to find Kim's cottage in the dark. He pulled his rental car off the road far enough away so as not to be conspicuous. Randy had given Peter all of Kim's things, and Will had driven her car from The Overlook, following Peter. He stopped to let Peter hop in and they drove down the long driveway. The house was dark. Peter let himself in and put the porch light on. They looked around. No one was there yet. They put Kim's bedroom light on so it would look like she was home. Then they waited in the darkened living room, listening for a car.

It wasn't long before they heard a truck on the drive. It stopped, and they heard the door slam. Peter and Will got ready. The storm door opened and he stepped into the room. Will shone his flashlight in his face while Peter closed the door, barring him from exiting.

"Why you son of a bitch," Will said, looking at Buck.

"What's up, bro? What're you doin' here? Isn't your pretty little innkeeper enough for ya? Or are ya comin' back for the nice piece of ass you missed in high school?" Buck was blinded by the light but had recognized Will's voice.

"Buck, what are you doing here?" Will said through clenched teeth.

"It's a free country. Why? Jealous? Trying to get back a missed opportunity? You weren't takin' care of business back in the day, Willy, so somebody had to."

"What are you talking about?" Will asked.

"Here she was, prancing around our house in her cheerleader uniform, or half naked when your mom would let her spend the night in a guest room. You weren't tapping her, so I did."

"What? She didn't want to…"

"No, you're right, she didn't." Buck interrupted. "But I did anyway. She fought and cried at first but then she liked it. Ask her. Every time I did it to her she called me Will. She still does. I figured it made her feel better, like she wasn't cheatin' or somethin'. I was just getting' her warmed up for ya…"

Will heard a dull thud and saw Buck's eyes roll back in his head. He slowly fell to the floor with a deafening thump.

143

"Sick son of a bitch." Peter Edgeworth was standing over Buck with a fireplace poker.

Sheriff Grady handcuffed Buck to the stretcher the EMTs had put him on, and notified the State Police he was on his way to the hospital. He made arrangements for Will and Peter to give their statements. Buck was screaming about pressing charges for assault as they wheeled him away.

"Peter, I know this has been a long time coming," the sheriff said. Peter nodded.

"You knew?" Will asked them.

"Yup. Suspected at least. When Peter found out Kim had been raped he called me. They'd moved away by then, but Peter always had his suspicions about Buck. I've kept an eye on him but it's been hard to catch him red handed with anything. And no one else ever reported sexual assault."

"Mr. E., Kim visited Faith at the inn, our old house. If that's where Buck..." Will stopped.

"God, I wonder if that was one of her triggers?" Peter asked.

"Yeah, going back to the place... Wait, he admitted it to us, but couldn't he retract his statement? How likely it is he'll be convicted? Especially if Kim isn't able to testify? Or won't?" Will asked.

"Well, that's where Peter and I got smart. Kim was pregnant," said the sheriff.

Will looked shocked.

"She miscarried. But because of the circumstances we had the Maryland State Police take my statement and a DNA sample from the baby. Buck didn't have any DNA in the system, and there was no probably cause to pick him up and test him. Kim didn't want to press charges, she wasn't strong enough. But now we have Buck, we have his DNA on this fireplace poker, and we have the DNA from Kim's unborn child. With our statements I think we have a good case against him," Peter said, nodding.

THIRTY ONE

Ciaran received a status update about Kim Edgeworth. Randy Preston said it would be a long time, according to her father, before Kim would be in any shape to return to work.

"Tell her father there will be a job waiting for her when she's better. And we'll continue to pay her medical benefits. All employees have sick leave and all that, hopefully she'll be right as rain by the time it runs out. We'll cross that bridge when we come to it," Ciaran told him.

Ciaran relayed what he knew to his 'family', now including Faith, Patty and Jack.

"Poor Kim," Faith said. "I can't imagine what she's going through. Or what her father's going through. I wonder if this had all started when she came to see me?" Patty rubbed Faith's back.

"She visited you? Why?" Ciaran asked. Faith told him the story.

"I'm sorry you went through all that, lass. That's not how CLI operates, so we'll chalk it up to Kim's illness. She was very bright and good at her job. Hopefully we'll be able to get her back to it someday."

Faith heard the main door open and stood to greet any arriving guests. Will walked into the bar with Peter Edgeworth. Jack jumped up.

"Peter, I'm so sorry to hear about Kim. I wish you were visiting under different circumstances," Jack said, shaking Peter's hand.

Ah, Faith thought, Kim's father. Jack made introductions all around. Will looked exhausted.

"Mr. Edgeworth, may I offer you anything? On the house, of course," Faith asked.

"Yes, I would love a drink. But not before offering you an apology."

"For what?"

"Mr. E., Faith doesn't know the whole story. She doesn't know why you're apologizing," Will stated. "Faith, can we talk?"

Faith asked her mom to get Mr. Edgeworth a drink and walked into the library with Will. He pulled her down on the sofa next to him.

"The biggest mistake I've ever made in my life was telling you we were through," he started. Faith teared up. "What Mr. E. was apologizing for was the horrible threats that Kim made to you, and the sexting she was doing to me."

"What?"

"I broke it off with you because I thought Kim was going to hurt you." Will pulled out his phone and showed the texts to Faith, all of them, the threats and the suggestive, lewd ones as well. She scrolled though them.

"Oh my God," she gasped.

"I have had nothing to do with Kim Edgeworth, and I don't want to have anything to do with her." Will relayed where he'd been that day and what he knew about Kim's hospitalization, the rape, the DNA test, the trap he and Mr. E. had set, and Buck.

Faith was horrified.

"And to think he was here most every night, what if..." She shivered.

"I know. The State Police are getting his trucking logs to see if any sexual assaults were reported in the towns he stopped at on the days of his runs. If there is even one woman who can testify... Sandy said he's not sure Kim will ever be able to testify, or that she won't always think we had a sexual relationship. But Mr. E. said she swore back then that I wasn't her attacker. And thankfully they have DNA that rules me out. I just feel so sorry for her, and for Mr. E."

"If it's any consolation, Da, um, Ciaran Lynch told her boss there will be a job for her when she's able to come back. And they'll take care of her benefits so she can get whatever care she needs. Hopefully he's telling Mr. Edgeworth that right now," Faith said.

"That will be a load off of his mind. Oh, and there was an envelope in her desk that had a lot of your financial stuff in it." Will had been holding it when he came in, and he'd laid it on the sofa table as they talked. He handed it to her. Faith furrowed her brows as she looked inside.

"These went missing a couple of weeks ago! I'd printed them out and had them on my desk. I thought they'd just been thrown away!"

"I'm guessing Buck lifted them and gave them to Kim," he said.

Will took the envelope from Faith and placed it back on the table. He took Faith's hands and looked into her eyes.

"I love you, Faith Nicholas. And I want you. But I'll wait forever if I have to. You are... the woman of my dreams." Will pulled her toward him and kissed her. "Literally. I dream about you every night," he said, resting his forehead against hers.

Faith realized she loved him, too. So what was she waiting for? The hotel business was always going to be crazy, would waiting to start her relationship with Will really make anything any different? She looked deep into his eyes and kissed him.

"I love you," she whispered. She could feel him smile as they kissed.

"I'll never get tired of hearing that," he whispered back.

THIRTY TWO

The Jay Feather Inn was full for Thanksgiving, including the recently finished and quickly appointed ski lodge. But all of the guests were visiting local family for the holiday, including Ciaran, Marthe and Brendan who had agreed to spend Thanksgiving with Faith.

After breakfast she'd set the dining room up with one long table for her Thanksgiving dinner guests. Will, Tom, and their parents, Jack, Patty, Iris, Gus, Sandy, Ciaran, Marthe, and Brendan. Kendra had promised to pop by to hang with Brendan after dinner at her grandmother's. And Sandy was bringing food to Kim and her father when he left for the hospital later in the day.

Patty and Faith were doing all the cooking as they'd given Delroy the day off to spend with Taylor and her family. Two dry-brined turkeys were in the oven along with a honey mustard glazed ham. The gravy had been made the day before using the turkey wings, and was now bubbling on the top of the stove. Roasted acorn squash, carrots and turnips, pearl onions with bacon and blue cheese, chestnuts and wild mushrooms in marsala, Patty's famous mashed potatoes and Faith's cranberry chutney rounded out the menu.

The group was scattered throughout the great room, library, bar and kitchen, helping or hindering, stealing kisses, chatting, and enjoying cocktails and hors d'oeuvres. All of the fireplaces were burning brightly, sending a welcome warmth through the inn on this cloudy, grey day.

Gus was munching on a celery stick stuffed with cream cheese and green olives.

"Muriel used to make these. They're my favorites," he said with a grin.

"I know," Faith said, winking at Sandy, "a little birdie told me."

Faith heard Iris giggle and saw Tom pull her into the library. Tanya and Jerry were thrilled that Tom was seeing Iris. As Faith walked through the inn with paté and crackers on a tray Will stole up behind her and kissed her neck.

"Hey, I'm workin' here!" she joked.

"Sorry, I can't help myself. I just keep thinking about last night..."

They hadn't had their normal goodnights since he'd told her they'd just keep it professional. She'd missed him, and the first quiet moment they'd had together had been last night after the inn's guests were in bed and the Taproom had closed. It was too cold to make out on his truck's tailgate, so they had snuck into the library to say goodnight. He'd pulled her onto his lap and couldn't get his lips on hers fast enough. His kisses were long and deep. She moaned quietly as he caressed her face and worked his way down to her breast. She could feel her arousal, and his. She got off of his lap.

"No, no, noooo. Where are you going?" His whisper sounded hurt. She walked to the door of the library, closed and locked it. His eyebrows rose. She walked back to the sofa and stood over him. She wasn't sure she was doing the right thing, but she went for it anyway.

"I don't want to wait anymore. I want you." She slipped off her sweater and slid off her jeans, standing before him in a nude lace bra and bikinis. He reached up and pulled her down on top of him. No questions asked.

He quickly dispatched with her lingerie and his clothes and was fondling her breasts, kissing her, whispering to her.

"I've waited so long to feel you like this. Oh, Beautiful, I'm gonna make you feel so good..."

Faith was hot and ready. She teased his tongue with her own, felt his sex and stroked him, and finally couldn't stand it any longer. She pulled him on top of her and he looked down at her and smiled.

"I want *you*," he said with a wicked grin as he slid into her. She gasped with delight and moaned softly. They found their rhythm and moved to each other's breath, each stroke, each thrust bringing them closer to paradise.

"I told you you'd be all mine," he whispered, watching her writhe.

Faith could feel her climax starting in her toes, the tingling moving up her body like lightening, until her back arched and her cries of pleasure overtook her. Will could stand it no longer as her ecstasy drove him to climax.

"Faith, oh God, Faith, that was..." Will panted.

"Yeah, it was..." Faith whispered back.

Will knew it was going to be a long day if he kept thinking about last night, but he couldn't help himself. And

149

here she was all beautiful in velvet pants and a silk blouse, and God knows what underneath; he just wanted to pet and fondle her all day. He'd have to make due with the occasional stolen kiss. She put the tray down and in front of God and country planted a long, slow kiss on Will's lips.

The hooting and hollering ramped up to a fair ruckus as everyone caught sight of that smooch. In all the excitement no one had heard the front door open.

"Young man, what do you think you're doing to my granddaughter?"

The room went silent. The woman stood in the doorway, an elegant coach suitcase on the floor next to her. She was Faith's height with snow-white hair in a chic chignon, wore a St. John knit suit in winter white with pearl buttons, and had a full-length mink coat over her shoulders. She was removing her gloves, surveying the room.

"GRAM!" Faith shouted, running to her with her arms wide. They embraced as Jack rushed to the door and caught her coat before the expensive fur hit the floor. There was much cooing and oohing and aahing between the women.

Iris ran into the kitchen to get Patty. In a loud stage whisper she said, "YOUR MOTHER IS HERE!!!"

"WHAT?" Patty flew to the foyer. "I thought you were in Majorca?" Patty said, kissing her mother and giving her a hug.

"It's Thanksgiving, the first one without your father. I thought I was fine, but I'm not. I wanted to be with family. I can't just keep traveling to run away from my grief."

"I'm so glad you came, Gram!" Faith hugged her again. "Let me introduce everyone." Faith walked her grandmother over to Will. "This is Will Grant. Will, this is Marjorie Nicholas, my grandmother."

She shook his hand.

"Yes, now I know who you are, but what are you? Boyfriend? Lover? Roll in the hay?" she asked.

Will blushed.

"Well, I was going to wait until later, but I guess I'll just go with the flow..."

Will got on one knee and pulled a stunning diamond ring out of his pocket. Faith was shocked. Her heart was racing and all the blood had left her head. She thought she might faint.

"Faith Nicholas, will you marry me?" Will's handsome face was glowing with love. The crowd around them went wild. Hank began to howl. "Just so you know, I did ask your father's permission," he added.

"Yes! Oh, yes!" She replied. He slid the ring on her finger, rose and pulled her into a long, deep kiss.

"Father?" Marjorie asked. "What father?"

Ciaran stepped forward. "Mrs. Nicholas that would be me, Ciaran Lynch. Happy to make your acquaintance."

Marjorie looked him up and down.

"So you're the one who knocked up my daughter thirty years ago."

Patty dropped her head and shook it, totally embarrassed.

"I think I'm going to like this woman," Marthe said.

Jack figured what the hell, this couldn't get much worse.

"Mrs. Nicholas, I'm Jack Kimball. I'm the one she's sleeping with now." He stuck his hand out. She shook it, threw her head back and laughed.

"Faith, you've managed to amass quite the cast of characters here. Do you have room for me?"

Iris had already set another place at the table. Next to Gus.

Faith barely remembered the meal. She was floating on air, looking at the perfect, beautiful ring on her hand. She and Will kept steeling glances and holding hands under the table. After dinner Jack put the football game on the TV in the Taproom, and some impromptu card games and board games began. Kendra dropped in and Brendan filled her in on all the news, and after she finished ogling Faith's ring Brendan dragged Kendra away to join a scrabble game with Iris and Tom in front of the fire.

Will pulled Faith into the library, shut the door and kissed her.

"Wow." He said to her, smiling.

"Wow, yourself. How long had you been planning that?" she asked.

"I bought the ring the week I met you. I've known all along you're the one. But Hank knew before me." He grinned. "Too fast?" he asked.

151

"No. I love you, I know that for sure. But we have to figure things out, like where will we live?"

"Details, details," he said as he kissed her again.

THIRTY THREE

The O'Dell Christmas Festival was just a few days away and the organizers still had not found a Mrs. Claus. They could certainly have made do with just Santa, but the festival had never been without the couple and some deemed it would be bad luck.

The weather had cooperated. Dan and Will had managed to get all of the tents up and the entire infrastructure in place before it snowed. And did it snow. Beautiful, soft flakes, not too wet, dry enough to dust off the steps with a broom. Seven inches of beautiful, twinkling snow. It lay upon the festival's Christmas Tree in the center of the green, making the lights sparkle even brighter.

Gus had been coming to the inn most every night for a drink. Sandy would bring him, or Will, or Jack. He always managed to make sure someone could swing by to get him and bring him home. But this night no one had heard from him, they all thought perhaps it was the snow that was keeping him home. Faith was getting ready to call him, just to check on him. But at about seven o'clock, before she made the call and while dinner was being served Faith heard a noise. Horns blowing. And bells. Sleigh bells! She ran to the window and saw a red sleigh drawn by two horses making it's way up the drive. Cars were flashing their lights and blowing their horns in salute, but all Faith could think was, the poor horses! All that noise!

Faith alerted the diners and those in the bar that a sleigh was coming up the drive. Festival vendors, families, Marjorie, Patty, Jack, and Will all gathered on the porch. Marthe and Brendan came out of the library.

"Too bad Da's not here to see this," Brendan said to Faith. She put her arm around him.

"I know! Not back from the office yet?" she asked. He shook his head.

The smaller kids were pointing and shouting, "It's Santa Claus!"

But as they came closer they saw that it was Ciaran at the reins. Marthe laughed and clapped. Brendan jumped up and down.

"Brilliant, Da!!"

As they drew up to the inn they saw Santa in the sleigh, holding a sign. It was Gus. He held the sign up. It said, "Marjorie, will you be Mrs. Claus?"

"What is that old fool up to?" Marjorie asked. Patty and Faith knew her annoyance was faked. Patty prodded her mother forward. "In the snow?" she asked Patty.

"Mom, the steps and the driveway are bare. You're not going to break a hip."

Jack had grabbed her mink from her room and placed it over Marjorie's shoulders.

"Sucking up, eh Jack?" she asked.

"Every chance I get, Marjorie."

He followed her to the sleigh, and he and Ciaran helped her get in beside Gus. Ciaran settled a fur throw over their legs.

Iris ran down the steps with a flask and two whiskey glasses.

"Good girl," Ciaran said to her.

"Do you want a glass?" she asked.

"No, I'm drivin'." He smiled and gave her a wink.

Gus looked at Marjorie and took her hand.

"You know, I wasn't coming down here every night just for the whiskey," he said earnestly.

"You weren't, huh?" she said, looking askance. "So is this for me? Or for the festival?"

"You. The festival just means I get to spend more time with you." He took her hand and squeezed it.

"Okay, then, I'll be your Mrs. Claus."

"Where are the rest of my girls?" he asked. Patty and Faith made their way to the sleigh. They gave both Marjorie and Gus pecks on the cheek.

"Your girls, eh?" Ciaran joked. Ciaran motioned for Marthe to join him and he hoisted her up to his perch. He climbed up beside her and took the reins, leading the horses in a circle and back down the drive.

"Yes. St. Nicholas's girls!" Gus shouted.

"Don't wait up!" Marjorie yelled.

EPILOGUE

The O'Dell Christmas Festival had record attendance that year. The money raised for The Children's Refuge indeed bought toys, Christmas dinner, and paid the winter heating bill, but it also bought new boots, coats and books for the home as well. Iris's bowls filled with Faith's soup sold out, but Iris took orders for additional bowls if people paid in advance, making extra money for the charity.

Marjorie kept the kids waiting to see Santa on the straight and narrow. It was the most expeditious line in the history of O'Dell's Christmas Festival. She'd shoot Gus a look if he was taking too long, and he'd just wink at her, giving the child as much time as he wanted.

Tom and Iris worked next to each other in adjoining booths at the festival, and moved in together soon after. They chose Tom's house, which he bought from Will, so Iris could set up her studio in the barn. Tom bought her a new kiln for Christmas.

Peter Edgeworth took Kim back to Maryland and the care of Dr. Roth. Her medication was changed to the drug Sandy Gregson had tried on her, which had fewer side effects and she tolerated well. She eventually returned to CLI, but chose to remain close to Baltimore and her doctor.

The State Police found three women who had been sexually assaulted by Buck. Because they had reported the crime and had been processed as victims the perpetrator's DNA was in the criminal justice system. Buck was convicted of four counts of aggravated assault and rape, and was sent to the Southern State Correctional Facility.

Dr. Roth was so impressed by Dr. Sandy Gregson that he offered him a position at his prestigious practice. Sandy moved to Maryland, and, as he was no longer her doctor of record, began dating Kim Edgeworth.

Marjorie bought a condo nearby, so she could spend time with Gus without the damned blue jay and cardinal squawking at them. But the birds followed them.

Jack took a tip from Will, and on Christmas Eve in front of her family and friends he took a knee and proposed to Patty with an emerald and diamond ring. Marjorie's comment was, "It's about time." They eloped on New Year's Eve in Quebec.

The Lynches stayed for Christmas, and a lot longer. Ciaran realized he missed his publican days and could be found most nights behind the bar in the Taproom, schmoozing guests and giving Iris his tips. When he flew his parents over to meet their second grandchild Ciaran's Da would join him behind the bar as well. Iris really cleaned up on those nights.

And Will and Faith? One year later, on Faith's birthday, Christmas Day, they were married at The Jay Feather Inn. Patty and Ciaran gave her away. Jack officiated. Hank was the ring bearer. Instead of wedding gifts they asked for donations to The Children's Refuge. Will collected all of the cash and checks and put them into a Christmas card to send to the charity. He signed it, "With Love from Saint Nicholas's Girls.

END

Jamaican Slang used in *St. Nicholas's Girls*

Ya Mon means yes, man or ma'am

Irie means everything is all right

Ag-o-ny means sexual orgasm

Mos Def means most definitely

Mash It Up means be a big success

Respect is a very popular Rasta greeting that shows courtesy

Me A Go means I am going

Soon Come means will be back, but not necessarily promptly

Dear Readers,

If you enjoyed *St. Nicholas's Girls* I hope you will leave a review at Amazon.com. I write these stories for all of you to enjoy, and the best way to spread the word is with your reviews. You have my undying gratitude.

All the Best,

D.P. McHenry

Other Works by D.P. McHenry

Never in My Life

Have you ever fallen hard for an unreachable rock star? What if he fell in love right back?

New Englander Kate Margaux is a crackerjack businesswoman in a stale relationship. Caught up in her dreams of a more exciting romantic life, she writes a novel about meeting the rock star of her fantasies, thinly veiling his identity. Her romance about fictional businesswoman Johanna and international rocker Ian becomes an overnight bestseller. But her real life British rock star, Simon Hardwicke, seeks out Kate after reading about the character he recognizes as himself. Fodder for the tabloids, Simon's pursuit of Kate wreaks havoc with Kate's relationship with her significant other and exposes Kate to an old lover whose obsession with Kate could turn deadly.

Is Simon drawn to Kate or the woman in her novel? Sparks fly, but is it love, lawsuit, or murder?

A Place Within Her

After a series of tragedies leaves her reeling, Thea Garrett escapes to the Caribbean to restart her life. Her photography business is booming, she is surrounded by the beauty of the islands, dances to reggae music on the beach and falls into bed with Nevisian Police Chief Peter Moses. But Thea witnesses the attempted kidnapping of British businessman Jasper Collins. A bond forms between his daughter Tori and Thea, and Jas is smitten with his daughter's new friend. Thea's affair with Peter, her growing relationship with Jasper Collins, and her friendship with Tori put Thea in the abductors' sights.

Can she protect Tori? And can Thea survive?

About the Author

D.P. McHenry is a romance writer who makes her home in New England, and writes about the places she knows and loves. She is also a blogger, whose website is home to her rants on food, life, love and travel.

Visit her at deborahdishes.com.

www.ingramcontent.com/pod-product-compliance
Lightning Source LLC
Chambersburg PA
CBHW070331130626
46556CB00007B/2803